ROPING

THE
RODEO QUEEN

Other Books by Anna Durand

Fastball Fever (All-American Men, Book One)
One Hot Chance (Hot Brits, Book One)
One Hot Roomie (Hot Brits, Book Two)
One Hot Crush (Hot Brits, Book Three)
The Dixon Brothers Trilogy (Hot Brits, Books 1-3 + Bonus Chapters)
One Hot Escape (Hot Brits, Book Four)
One Hot Rumor (Hot Brits, Book Five)
One Hot Christmas (Hot Brits, Book Six)
One Hot Scandal (Hot Brits, Book Seven)
One Hot Deal (Hot Brits, Book Eight)
One Hot Favor (Hot Brits, Book Nine)
One Hot Bash (Hot Brits, Book Ten)
One Hot Moment (Hot Brits, Book Eleven)
One Hot Chase (Hot Brits, Book Twelve)
The American Wives Club (A Hot Brits/Hot Scots/Au Naturel Crossover)
Brit vs. Scot (A Hot Brits/Hot Scots/Au Naturel Crossover)
A Novel Secret (A Hot Brits/Hot Scots/Au Naturel Crossover)
Dangerous in a Kilt (Hot Scots, Book One)
Wicked in a Kilt (Hot Scots, Book Two)
Scandalous in a Kilt (Hot Scots, Book Three)
The MacTaggart Brothers Trilogy (Hot Scots, Books 1-3)
Gift-Wrapped in a Kilt (Hot Scots, Book Four)
Notorious in a Kilt (Hot Scots, Book Five)
Insatiable in a Kilt (Hot Scots, Book Six)
Lethal in a Kilt (Hot Scots, Book Seven)
Irresistible in a Kilt (Hot Scots, Book Eight)
Devastating in a Kilt (Hot Scots, Book Nine)
Spellbound in a Kilt (Hot Scots, Book Ten)
Relentless in a Kilt (Hot Scots, Book Eleven)
Incendiary in a Kilt (Hot Scots, Book Twelve)
Wild in a Kilt (Hot Scots, Book Thirteen)
Unstoppable in a Kilt (Hot Scots, Book Fourteen)
Valentine in a Kilt (Hot Scots, Book Fifteen)
Electrifying in a Kilt (Hot Scots, Book Sixteen)
The Notorious Dr. MacT (A Hot Scots Prequel)
The British Bastard (A Hot Scots Prequel)
Natural Obsession (Au Naturel Nights, Book One)
Natural Deception (Au Naturel Nights, Book Two)
Natural Temptation (Au Naturel Nights, Book Three)
Natural Passion (Au Naturel Trilogy, Book One)
Natural Impulse (Au Naturel Trilogy, Book Two)
Natural Satisfaction (Au Naturel Trilogy, Book Three)
Lachlan in a Kilt (The Ballachulish Trilogy, Book One)
Aidan in a Kilt (The Ballachulish Trilogy, Book Two)
Rory in a Kilt (The Ballachulish Trilogy, Book Three)

ROPING THE RODEO QUEEN

All-American Men, Book Two

ANNA DURAND

JACOBSVILLE BOOKS • CHESTERHILL, OHIO

ROPING THE RODEO QUEEN

ISBN: 978-1-964417-47-9 (paperback)
ISBN: 978-1-964417-48-6 (ebook)
ISBN: 978-1-964417-49-3 (retail audiobook)
ISBN: 978-1-964417-50-9 (library audiobook)

Library of Congress Control Number: 2025913014

Manufactured in the United States.

Jacobsville Books
www.JacobsvilleBooks.com

Publisher's Cataloging-in-Publication Data
provided by Five Rainbows Cataloging Services

Names: Durand, Anna.
Title: Roping the rodeo queen : a rodeo romance / Anna Durand.
Description: Chesterhill, OH : Jacobsville Books, 2025. | Series: All-American men, bk. 2.
Identifiers: LCCN 2025914865 | ISBN 978-1-964417-47-9 (paperback) | ISBN 978-1-964417-48-6 (ebook) | ISBN 978-1-964417-49-3 (retail audiobook) | ISBN 978-1-964417-50-9 (library audiobook)
Subjects: LCSH: Cowboys--Fiction. | Cowgirls--Fiction. | Rodeo performers--Fiction. | Rodeos--Fiction. | Man-woman relationships--Fiction. | Romance fiction. | BISAC: FICTION / Romance / Sports. | FICTION / Romance / Contemporary. | GSAFD: Love stories.
Classification: LCC PS3604.U724 R67 2025 (print) | LCC PS3604.U724 (ebook) | DDC 813/.6--dc23.

Chapter One

Dust and Determination

What a beautiful day for a rodeo in the beautiful city of Tampa, Florida. I'm standing beside my trusty mount, Black Thunder, a horse who has more sense than half the cowboys I know. While I push the curry comb through his coat, it releases any dirt and loose hair. Can't have my big buddy looking shabby. Then I switch to the dandy brush to create a sleek shine that will look outstanding in the arena. With every stroke of the brush, I fall into a rhythm that's as familiar as the lines on my palm.

"Looking sharp, Thunder." I pat him on the rump. "Nobody's more handsome than you. All the mares and fillies told me so."

The big guy nickers in response, as if he agrees with my statement. We've been through enough rodeos to know the drill. His coat gleams in the sun, and his muscles ripple beneath his skin as I lead him away from our trailer. But it's not our turn in the ring yet. So, I turn my attention to my tack. Three years ago, I spent a long time and a tidy sum to find the perfect saddle. It is a fine piece of craftsmanship, for sure. Lately, my dad has started to signal that he thinks I should buy a new saddle. But the slightly worn leather suits me perfectly, like a well-loved pair of boots. I glide my hands over the seat, checking for any wear and tear, my fingers as nimble as a pickpocket at a county fair. I slide my fingers down the stirrups too, checking for any wear and tear. Satisfied, I pat the saddle.

"Couldn't do this without you, buddy. You're my secret weapon, right?" I chuckle at my own words, giving the saddle a final pat before moving on to the reins. They're sturdy and reliable—a lot like me—or so I've been told by ladies who appreciate a man who knows his way around a lasso.

"Every loop, every knot, has gotta be perfect," I remind myself, because when you're hurtling through the dirt at breakneck speed, perfection isn't just for show, it's survival. And let's face it, second place is just the first loser. "Clay McKendrick ain't in the business of losing. Not today, not ever."

Okay, most people think I'm weird for chatting to my horse the way I do. Who cares? Thunder isn't just a horse. He's my best friend.

As I loop the reins over Thunder's neck, I tune out most of the cacophony around me here at the Tampa Rodeo and Family Festival. The noise of the crowd swells like a distant ocean, punctuated by the occasional bellow from the loudspeaker—a sponsor's spiel about chewy jerky or the latest in cowboy boot fashion. It's all white noise to me, just another layer of the rodeo soundscape that fades into the background. But the chatter of a couple cowboys breaks through my Zen zone.

"Hey, did you hear about that new barrel racer girl?" one guy asks his buddy. "They say she's fire in the ring but ice everywhere else. No time for dating. She just eats, sleeps, and breathes rodeo."

His cohort snorts, almost like a horse. "Yeah, she's uppity for sure. I waved hi to her earlier, and she totally froze me out. What a bitch."

I can't help but smirk, my eyes rolling skyward like I'm searching for divine patience. Seems like every year there's a fresh face with the same old story about some girl who didn't go for his so-called charms. You'd think these guys had never seen a woman who's determined to win before. Not that I'm one to gossip. I reckon my horse chats more than I do on competition days. Thunder loves to nicker at the cute mares.

"Focus, Clay," I mutter under my breath, checking the cinch one last time, making sure it's snug against Thunder's belly without pinching. Old habits die hard, and the itch for perfection keeps me sharp—even if the idle banter of those cowboys annoys me.

The first guy pipes up again. "That filly is probably too high maintenance, anyway."

"More like too busy kicking your ass to care," I retort quietly, only half-joking. There's nothing quite like a bit of friendly competition to get the blood pumping. But today, I've got my own race to run, and no amount of hot gossip is going to throw me off course. Not by a long shot. Took me years to work my way up to the pro circuit—the PRCA, or Professional Rodeo Cowboy Association. Cowgirls compete here too.

The din of the crowd swells like waves in an Olympic swimming pool. But it's just background noise to me. I've got my eyes on the prize and my mind set on the tight turns and the clock that doesn't care about anyone's drama. The boys can yak all they want about the latest queen of the barrels, but my focus is sharper than the spurs on my boots.

"Clayton McKendrick, you're here to ride, not gossip," I remind myself, a grin tugging at my lips. Lord knows my old man would have my hide if he caught me getting distracted by anything less than a bull with a vendetta.

I give Thunder a final pat, the solid muscle beneath his shiny coat a reassuring feeling, and I raise my head to survey the arena. And that's when I see *her*—Jolene Callahan. I've heard she prefers to be called Jo, but I can't deny I like her full name. It sounds like a challenge, something wild and untamed. She stands across the arena, a good stone's throw away, but distance ain't nothing when someone like the former rodeo queen commands the space.

She swiftly wrangles that long, auburn hair into a neat ponytail, lacing her fingers through the strands with the kind of intent I reserve for tying down a calf. Her expression is stoic as she studies the entire arena, even checking out the folks in the crowd. Now that's determination.

"Steady there, cowboy," I whisper, but it's not Thunder needing the reminder. It's me. I can't resist tracking Jo's every move, the way she rolls her shoulders back and lifts her chin slightly. Jolene Callahan is no delicate flower waiting to be plucked. She's the storm you chase on the horizon, knowing full well you might get swept up in it.

Focus, Clay. I remind myself in my head, trying to stamp out the spark of interest that flares up unwelcome. *You've got a job to do, so stick to it.* But even as I think those words, I feel an itch beneath my skin that has nothing to do with saddle sores or the dust of the arena.

Jo is no ordinary girl. She's the kind who can swat away a man's advances with one finger and who probably thinks men like me are simply barrels getting in her way. But damn if that doesn't make her all the more intriguing. Miss Callahan has the kind of body any man would love to explore for hours, under the sheets. I'd love to be the one to tame her wild instincts and rein her in for a night—or maybe longer. She has the best tits in the rodeo world, not to mention those slender yet strong thighs. To have my dick between them, pushing inside her body…Shit, I'm already getting hot just thinking about it.

"McKendrick?"

I blink several times, and it's only then do I realize I'm not alone. One of the event organizers, Jake Walsh, stands beside me. He holds a clipboard, seeming equal parts curious and impatient.

"Sorry, Jake," I reply with a tip of my hat. "Just admiring the competition."

"Right," he drawls, clearly unconvinced. "So that's what they call it these days when a cowboy sees something he likes."

He winks, his gaze drifting to Jo Callahan briefly. "Better saddle up, Clay."

"Right," I agree, but I'm not really talking to anyone. I'm speaking to myself, to the part of me that can't seem to look away from Jolene Callahan—the barrel racer who's probably more dangerous than any bronc I'm about to ride. I'm here to make my mark and earn enough money to pay my dad's medical bills.

Jake saunters away without glancing back.

Okay, enough dawdling. I turn back to Thunder, my loyal companion, who's as impatient as a child before Christmas morning—or so his hoof-stomping tells me.

With a firm grip, I hoist the saddle onto Thunder's back, ensuring the straps are tightened to perfection. Can't have any slip-ups now, not with so much at stake.

"Alrighty, time for one last check," I say, more to myself than to Thunder, who seems to understand the assignment without being told. With s thorough check, a twist here, a tug there, we're golden—or at least, as golden as a man can be when he's about to jump into a team roping event.

"Hey there, Clay!" someone shouts from behind, but I don't bother turning. If they've got legs, they can come find me on their own.

"Kinda busy, pal," I call out, not unkindly but with the tone of a man who's got bigger fish to fry—or rather, bigger animals to wrangle. I can't deny, there's a certain poetry to roping, a rhythm that gets my blood pumping just right.

I glance across the arena one more time, where Jo is now adjusting her gloves, a focused furrow etched between her brows. She's all business, for sure. But I reckon there's a fire inside her, the kind that could make a cowboy want to know what ignites her.

"Knock it off, McKendrick," I chide myself, shaking my head. There's no room for musing over barrel racers, no matter how intriguing or, well, fetching they might be.

I pat Thunder's neck. "Let's show 'em how it's done, hey?"

He snorts, and I swear he's agreeing with me. Or maybe I've just spent too much time around horses.

No, that's impossible.

I step into the stirrup and hoist myself up and onto the saddle. The leather softly creaks beneath my thighs, a sure sign I'm ready to go. This is where I belong, where all the chatter and gossip fades away, leaving only the timeless dance of man and beast, the roar of the crowd, and the sweet, sweet scent of competition in the air. I love the poetry of the rodeo.

"Alrighty, let's do this," I tell Thunder, who grunts his approval and shakes his head once.

Suddenly, the distinctive voice of Buck "Silver Tongue" Hawkins crackles over the PA system, announcing the next event. I'd know that gravelly drawl anywhere, even if I were deaf in one ear.

"Ladies and gentlemen, please direct your attention to the arena for our next event. Team roping is about to begin, and we've got some of the finest cowboys in the PRCA ready to show you what real coordination looks like!"

Yee-haw! Now the fun really starts.

Chapter Two

A Cowboy's Dream

The first sign that today might be my lucky day had come when my truck didn't die on the final stretch to Tampa, Florida. The second bit of good luck occurred when Buck Hawkins greeted me. He was the first person I saw when I pulled into the parking lot.

"Well, I'll be damned. If it isn't Clay McKendrick in the flesh." Buck's voice booms across the parking area. His wide grin makes me smile too as I ease my weathered Ford F-150 into a spot. The horse trailer rattles along behind me. "Thought you might've changed your mind, son."

I kill the engine and hop out, boots hitting the dusty ground with a familiar thud. "Takes more than a busted radiator and three flat tires to keep me away from Tampa."

Buck's laughter is contagious, infecting me too as he strides over to me. His signature silver belt buckle catches the waning sunlight. At fifty-five, the man still commands attention like he was born for it. Well, he is the most recognizable voice in rodeo.

"Kid, you look like you've been drug through hell backwards." Buck claps his hand on my shoulder, and I catch the faint scent of bourbon on his breath. Not unusual for Buck, especially when the pressure of a big event has him wound tight. "But you made it, Clay, and that's what counts."

"Barely made it." I pull off my hat and run a hand through my hair, still damp with sweat from the nerve-racking drive. "Lost two days waiting for parts in Tallahassee, then had to sweet-talk a mechanic into working Sunday just to get the trailer hitch fixed."

"All that matters is you're here now." Buck studies my face, his eyes as sharp as ever despite the years. "You still set on this PRCA dream of yours?"

The question catches me off guard. I've been chasing that dream for three years now, ever since Dad's medical bills started piling up and the bank started making noises about foreclosure. The McKendrick Ranch has been in our family for four generations, and I'll be damned if I'll be the one to lose it.

"More than ever," I tell Buck, settling my hat back on my head. "The ranch won't save itself, and the amateur circuit won't pay the bills."

Buck nods. "You know I'd help if I could."

"Of course you would, and I appreciate that." That man has known my family since I was knee-high to a grasshopper, and he watched me grow up riding everything that moved on four legs. I even tried to rope a deer once.

"The PRCA's a tough nut to crack, son. You sure you're ready for that kind of pressure?"

Before I can answer, the crunch of expensive boots on gravel makes us both turn. Brock Sterling swaggers past me, his pristine black hat tilting at just the right angle to catch the light. His hand-tooled boots probably cost more than I could make in three months. His shiny belt buckle gleams like it's never seen a day of honest work.

"Well, well, look what the cat dragged in." Brock's voice drips with both practiced charm and snide intentions. Somehow, that makes sponsors want to throw money at him. He rakes his gaze over my dusty jeans and scuffed boots with barely concealed disdain. "Clay McKendrick, right? Still riding with that old saddle of your Grand-daddy?"

My jaw tightens, but I keep my voice level. "You know damn well I got a new one three years ago."

"Sure you do, cowboy." He flashes that million-dollar smile that graces magazine covers. "Just remember, this ain't the county fair circuit anymore. Wouldn't want you to embarrass yourself out there."

Buck steps forward, his presence commanding enough to make even Brock Sterling pause. "You worry about your own riding, Sterling. I've seen Clay here bring the heat with times that'd make your fancy sponsors sweat."

Brock's smile doesn't falter, but something cold flickers behind his eyes. "Just making conversation, Buck. No need to get all defensive on the kid's behalf." He turns his attention back to me. "Looking forward to seeing what you've got, McKendrick. May the best man win."

The way he says it makes it clear who he thinks that is. Brock has an ego the size of North America.

As the jackass struts away toward a gleaming truck and trailer combo that probably cost more than my entire ranch, Buck spits on the ground. "Don't let that peacock get in your head. Sterling's got the backing and the gear, but I've seen him choke when the pressure's on."

"Doesn't matter." I watch Brock's retreating figure. "I didn't come here to worry about him. I came here to ride and win the cash prize."

But even as the words leave my mouth, I can feel that familiar knot of doubt twisting in my gut. Sterling's right about one thing—this isn't the county fair circuit. The PRCA is where careers are made and broken, where the difference between glory and going home empty-handed can come down to fractions of a second.

"That's the spirit." Buck's voice pulls me back from my spiraling thoughts. "Now, let's get your horse settled and go register you for the events."

I amble toward the trailer, grateful for something to do with my hands. The familiar routine of checking on my gelding helps to steady my nerves. Thunder pokes his head out as I approach, and I can't help but smile at his eager expression. At least one of us is excited to be here.

"Easy, boy," I murmur, running my hand along his neck. Thunder's been my partner for the better part of five years, and he knows the drill as well as I do. Maybe better. "We're gonna show these fancy jerks what real riding looks like."

Buck peers into the trailer, his experienced eye assessing my horse with the same intensity he brings to calling events. "He's looking good, Clay. Filled out since I saw him last spring."

"I've been working him hard for this competition." I unlatch the trailer door and back Thunder out slowly. The gelding's hooves ring against the metal ramp, and his ears prick as he takes in the sights and sounds of the rodeo grounds. "Figure if I'm gonna make my move, might as well do it right."

The late afternoon sun beats down on my neck as I lead Thunder across the dusty parking area. The smell of hay, manure, and fried food fills the air—the unmistakable scent of rodeo that's been in my blood since before I could walk.

"Registration closes in forty minutes," Buck reminds me, checking his watch. "Let's get this boy settled, and you signed up before Marlene at the desk goes on her dinner break. Woman's stricter than a drill sergeant about those deadlines."

I nod, adjusting my grip on Thunder's lead rope. "Stalls in the same place as last year?"

"Yep. East side, near the practice arena." Buck falls into step beside me, his slight limp barely noticeable unless you know to look for it. The old bronc riding injury from '98 ended his competitive career but launched him into announcing. "Got you one reserved, Clay. Pulled some strings with the event coordinator. You're welcome, by the way."

"Appreciate it." I glance at him sideways. "What'd that cost you?"

Buck waves a hand dismissively. "Just promised I'd mention her nephew's feed store during the broadcast. Kid's trying to compete with those big-box places. Could use the publicity."

That's Buck all over—always working some angle, trading favors like poker chips. But unlike most people in this business, he uses his connections to help others as often as himself.

We pass a row of gleaming trailers sporting sponsor logos and custom paint job that make my rusted rig look like it belongs in a junkyard. But I push the thought aside. Money doesn't ride the horse. Only skill can do that.

"I hear Sterling's got a new sponsor," Buck says, lowering his voice though there's nobody close enough to hear. "Some energy-drink company throwing cash at him like it's confetti. Word is they're paying him more than most cowboys make in five years just to wear their logo on his vest."

I shake my head, leading Thunder around a puddle of muddy water. "Must be nice to have cash thrown at you for looking pretty."

"Pretty don't stay on a bronc for eight seconds," Buck asserts, but there's something in his tone that tells me he's seen plenty of pretty boys with deep pockets outlast scrappy kids with heart. "Still, having that kind of backing takes the pressure off. A man doesn't have to worry about entry fees or truck payments when he's got corporate money rolling in."

The knot in my stomach tightens another notch. I've got exactly enough cash for my entry fees and maybe two meals that don't come from a vending machine. If I can't place this weekend, the drive home's gonna be a long one.

Thunder snorts and tosses his head, sensing my tension. I pat his neck, my gaze fixed on a group of riders gathered around the practice pen. They're all decked out in matching gear, laughing and slapping each other on the back like they belong to some exclusive club. Sponsor patches cover their vests like badges of honor.

"Well, would you look at that," Buck mutters. "Whole damn Energy Drink posse is here."

A lanky blonde guy spots us and nudges his buddy. They both stare for a second before turning back to their conversation, snickering. I've seen that look before—the quick assessment and dismissal. The unspoken judgment: *Not one of us.*

"Good luck tomorrow, Clay," Buck says, clapping me on the shoulder before heading off to meet with the event organizers.

I will try to give it everything I've got, no matter what the naysayers think. I have the best motivation ever.

Making my dad proud.

Chapter Three

Collision Course

The rhythmic pounding of hooves echoes through the arena, and I can't help being riveted by the sight. Jo Callahan is a blur of auburn hair coupled with a look of fierce determination as she careens around each barrel with the kind of precision that would make a Swiss watchmaker green with envy. I'm frozen just watching the former rodeo queen, unable to tear my gaze away from Jolene Callahan.

"Come on, Jo!" someone screams from the stands. But that person's voice is drowned out by the collective roar of the crowd.

I find myself silently cheering her on too. It's more than her skill that captivates me. Her relentless competitive spirit sets my heart to racing every time she rounds another barrel. Jo Callahan is suffused with firecracker energy that could light up all of Tampa. Who would've guessed that I, Clay McKendrick, would get so caught up in the spectacle.

As Jo rounds the final barrel and sprints towards the finish line, I lean forward on the railing, my own body tensing as if I'm the one in the saddle. As she crosses the line, Buck's excited voice crackles over the loudspeaker. "And that's a new arena record set by Jolene Callahan of the famed Callahan family of rodeo royalty!"

The entire arena erupts in a wall of deafening cheers. Yet there's Jo, dismounting her horse, as cool as a cucumber. Composure must be her middle name, or at least that's what she lets the world think. I can't stop watching her. She's amazing, and a fleeting thought rushes through my mind. What would it be like to make love to the rodeo queen?

"Bet she's got ice running through those veins," I whisper to no one in particular, a half-smile playing on my lips.

Yet a deeply buried part of me is itching to know if anyone's ever melted her icy core. Does she ever let down those guardrails and expose the raw, unfiltered side of Jolene Callahan? The thought of becoming the one who glimpses that side of her…it makes the hair on my arms shiver erect.

Still mesmerized, I watch Jo leading her horse away. She looks every bit the former Miss Rodeo Colorado. I'm alone at the edge of the arena, ruminating over records and walls coming down. *Jo Callahan, you're one heck of a puzzle—and I reckon I've never been good at riddles. But something tells me you might just be worth figuring out.*

While I strap on my chaps, I muse about the way worn leather almost smells better than food, and how I'd love to fuck Jo on a blanket with green grass beneath it. Yeah, it's definitely been way too long since I got any action. But I need to focus on the task at hand—getting ready for a hard ride. Every buckle slides into place with a familiar clicking sound that usually steadies my nerves. But this evening, I'm distracted. I fumble with the last fastening as Jo rounds the corner, heading for the stalls, paying no attention to me.

"Whoa" is all I can manage to say before we collide.

Her shoulder rams into my chest with enough force to send my hat flying.

"Jesus!" She stumbles backward, one hand still gripping her horse's reins, and shoots me a scathing look. "Are you planning on setting up camp in the middle of the walkway?"

Our eyes lock, and for a brief moment, I swear something gentler flickers behind that tough-as-nails façade. Maybe it's surprise or even a hint of embarrassment. But it's gone before I can be sure, replaced by that trademark Callahan stoicism.

"Congratulations on the record," I offer, bending to retrieve my hat. "That was impressive riding."

She tilts her head, studying me as if I'm a new species of rodeo creature she's never encountered before. Then she finally speaks, though her words are clipped. "Thanks, McKendrick. Good luck out there. Sounds like you might need it."

Before I can respond, Buck's voice booms over the loudspeaker. "Next up, folks, we've got Clay McKendrick from the McKendrick Ranch in Montana! This young man has been making a name for himself on the circuit, first as an amateur, and now as a pro. His father's accident kept him off the circuit for a spell, but now he's baaaack!"

Not sure my dad would enjoy hearing his problems aired out in public, but Buck means well. He visits the ranch at least twice a month.

Jo's expression shifts subtly. Is that…sympathy? Whatever it is, I don't want it, not from her.

"Better get out there," Jo suggests. She shuffles a little closer to me, her voice a touch softer than before. "They're waiting for you. And I'll be watching—from the stands."

I jam my hat back on my head and square my shoulders. Something about knowing that Jo will be watching me perform makes my stomach flutter in a very unmanly way.

"Don't worry about me," I assure her with more confidence than I feel. I'm not nervous about being in the spotlight. It's her presence that knocks me off kilter just a little. "I've been doing this since before I could walk straight, Callahan."

A hint of a smile plays at the corner of her mouth. "Never said I was worried."

Jo ambles toward the stalls.

As I swerve my attention back to the arena, I catch her glancing back at me repeatedly. *Interesting.* I push the thought aside and focus on what's ahead—sixty seconds that could make or break my week.

The crowd cheers for the roping team, which includes me and a few others. As I enter the arena, I settle into the saddle, not the least bit anxious. This is my home territory—the rodeo world. Thunder and I move as one unit within the whole team, muscles tense and ready to go.

Denny Garrison is my partner in the team roping event, a partnership that's worked for two years. Our roping team works like a well-oiled machine as the calf sprints out of the chute, and I'm right after it, rope swinging overhead in a perfect loop. The throw lands clean around the horns, and I dally the rope around my saddle horn with practiced precision. Denny's right where he needs to be, coming in from the side.

Six-point-eight seconds. Not bad, but not great either.

The crowd offers polite applause as we exit, and I know without looking at the leaderboard that it won't be enough to beat Sterling. His run with his partner had been virtually flawless, with six-point-two seconds of textbook roping that had the sponsors in the VIP section practically salivating.

"Solid run," Denny says, patting my back as we lead our horses away from the arena. "We'll get 'em next time."

As I exit the arena, Jo is still there, leaning against the fence with her arms crossed. Her horse stands patiently beside her with the reins looped over her arm. "Not bad, McKendrick."

"Faint praise, huh?" I saunter up to her, pulling off my gloves with more force than necessary. "You know what they say. Second place won't pay the bills, sweetheart."

The endearment slips out before I can squelch it.

"Could've fooled me." Her green eyes narrow as if she thinks she can humiliate me with the sly smile that's playing across her lips. But her expression softens. "Looked like you knew what you were doing out there."

"Knowing what I'm doing and getting it done are two different things." I wipe sweat from my forehead with the back of my hand, still wound tight from the adrenaline and disappointment. "Sterling's got this whole thing sewn up tighter than a tick on a hound dog."

Jo's horse nudges her shoulder, and she absently strokes the mare's neck. "You sound like a man who's already given up."

"Not by a long shot." I use adjusting my gloves as an excuse not to look at her. "I'm only stating facts. My first PRCA event went sideways. That's a fact."

"A fact?" Jo's eyebrow arches in that challenging way that makes me want to either walk away or step closer. I haven't decided which. "The fact is you're two-tenths of a second behind, not two minutes. That's nothing in the grand scheme of things."

I snort, adjusting my hat for no reason. "Easy for you to say, Callahan. You just set a new arena record."

"Yeah, after placing third in the last four events." She runs her fingers through her horse's mane, her gaze steady on mine. "You think I just woke up one morning and decided to be exceptional? This game is about persistence, McKendrick. Showing up even when you're beat to hell and just want to sleep for a month."

There's something in her voice, a raw honesty that catches me off guard. For a moment, the mask slips, and I glimpse something real beneath Jo Callahan's perfect exterior.

"I show up," I all but snarl through my teeth. "Every—damn—time."

Jo shakes her head. "Then stop acting like second place is the end of the world."

I roll my eyes. "You kinda suck at pep talks."

She steps closer, close enough that I catch the scent of leather and something floral. "You've got talent, McKendrick. Anyone with eyes can see that."

Coming from Jo Callahan, that's practically a declaration of undying admiration. I'm not sure how to respond, so I default to what I know—deflection. "Careful there, Callahan. Someone might think you're paying me a compliment."

Her lips quirk upward. "God forbid."

We stand here for a beat too long, the air between us charged with something I can't quite name. Her horse whickers softly, breaking the moment, and she leads her mount away.

Jo Callahan is beautiful. But no way can I ever get involved with her. *Focus on the goal, Clay, not the girl.*

I've got more important things to worry about.

Chapter Four

An Unlikely Alliance

Do I have any chance of winning even one big prize in the PRCA championships? I need the money, for sure, to keep my family's ranch afloat. But I feel like a pathetic excuse for a cowboy right now. Maybe I should just go home and find a real job as an accountant or…something.

The thought evaporates as soon as it enters my head. McKendricks don't quit. Dad always told us so, even when the doctors were certain he might never walk again after the accident. Even when the medical bills started piling up like tumbleweeds against a barbed wire fence. Dad's doing much better, but the bills won't disappear.

I shake my head and focus on untacking Thunder, letting the familiar routine calm my pissed-off attitude. The gelding nickers affectionately, sensing my mood. I pull a piece of carrot out of my pocket and offer it to him. He prefers carrots over store-bought treats.

A sigh whispers out of me. "At least one of us performed today. Wasn't me, though."

I check his legs for any signs of strain, but everything looks good. Thunder's as solid as they come, bred for endurance and heart rather than flash. Just like his rider, I suppose.

"Clay McKendrick, you sorry son of a bitch, get your head outta your ass."

I glance up from where I'm sitting on a hay bale behind the live-stock pens, wallowing in my own misery like a barnyard pig. Buck Hawkins stands there with his hands on his hips, looking madder than I've ever seen him.

"Buck, what's wrong?" I ask, sitting up straighter.

"Don't you 'Buck' me, boy. I just watched you ride like you belonged out there, and now you're sitting here moping like someone shot your dog." He shakes his head, frowning. "What's gotten into you?"

"Nothing. I'm sizing up my chances realistically." I stand up and dust off my jeans. "Second place won't win championships, and championships are what I need to save the ranch."

"Hell, son, you think every cowboy who ever made it big won their first rodeo?" Buck's weathered face softens just a touch. "This is one day out of a whole season. You're in this for the long haul. That's the only way to win."

I push a hand through my hair, frustration bubbling up like a mud pot. "Long haul doesn't mean much when the bank's breathing down your neck, Buck. I needed that win today."

"And you'll get it next time," he insists, with the sort of confidence I wish I could bottle and drink. "But not if you're sitting here feeling sorry for yourself instead of studying what went wrong."

My mouth opens, but I don't get the chance to speak. The sound of boots on gravel draws my attention.

Jo Callahan is approaching. Her eyes catch the late afternoon sun, making their emerald color seem to glitter like polished gems. My stomach does a weird little flip that I immediately blame on hunger.

"Gentlemen," Jo says with a curt nod to each of us. "Buck, they need you at the announcer's booth."

"Be there in a jiff." He glances at me and winks. "Don't worry so much, kid. Everything will pan out, trust me. Old Silver Tongue knows all."

Then he trots away, leaving me alone with Jolene Callahan.

She looks damn good—sexy as hell, actually—though all she's wearing is a pair of faded jeans and a pastel plaid shirt that hangs below her hips. I shouldn't get so turned on by that, but I am. Big time. I find myself wondering what it would be like to kiss that smart mouth of hers until she's breathless and so wet for me that the scent of her desire fills the air.

Christ, McKendrick. Get a grip.

Jo settles onto the hay bale beside me. "You look like somebody told you Christmas was canceled."

"Been thinking, that's all."

"Hmm, that could become a dangerous habit."

Is she flirting with me? Nah, she wouldn't do that. But Jo is close enough that her thigh brushes against mine—and my dick twitches in response. Christ, I hope she didn't notice that. I need to keep my voice steady, though having her this close makes my pulse kick up like a spooked horse.

Jo leans back on her hands, studying me with those keen eyes. "What's eating at you? And don't say 'nothing.' You've been wearing that storm cloud expression since you left the arena."

I debate whether to tell her the truth. Hell, half the rodeo circuit probably knows about my family's financial problems. It's hardly a secret. Most everyone has heard about my dad's injury.

"The ranch is in trouble," I finally admit while staring down at my boots. "Has been for a while now. Dad's medical bills after his accident…Well, let's just say they weren't covered by our insurance."

Her expression mutates into something that's almost tender. "How bad is it, Clay?"

"Bad enough that if I don't start placing first instead of second, we're gonna lose everything." The words taste bitter in my mouth. "Four generations of McKendricks have worked that land, and I'm about to be the jackass who lets it slip away."

She remains quiet for a long moment, and it feels like she's inspecting me—like I'm a prize bull. When I finally raise my head, I notice something unexpected in her gaze—calculation. Whatever she's up to now, I'm not sure I'll like it.

Jo leans toward me, crossing one leg over the other. "You know what your problem is, McKendrick?"

"I'm pretty sure you're about to tell me—whether or not I want to hear it."

"You're thinking too small, McKendrick." She stands up and brushes hay off her jeans. "Sponsors, that's what you need, Clay."

Did the rodeo ice queen just invoke my first name? That's…strange.

"Sponsors?" I let out a humorless laugh. "In case you haven't noticed, I'm not exactly Brock Sterling. Companies aren't lining up to throw money at me."

"They could be." She crosses her arms and widens her stance. "You've got the talent. What you lack is the story."

"The story," I repeat flatly. I've got no idea what she means.

"Yes, the story. The narrative. The thing that makes people want to root for you." Jo starts pacing, back and forth, back and forth. "Sterling has a pretty-boy image and family connections. What do you have that makes you stand out from the crowd?"

I shrug, feeling increasingly uncomfortable under her scrutiny. "I ride horses and bulls and rope calves. Same as everyone else here."

"God, you're dense." She halts directly in front of me, hands on her hips. "You are the underdog fighting to save his family's legacy. The fourth-generation rancher who refuses to give up. Clay McKendrick the guy who drove thousands of miles to get here because quitting isn't in your DNA." Her tone grows tougher with every word as passion lights up her features—passion for winning, that is. "That's a story people want to get behind, you stubborn ass."

I gape at her, caught off guard by the fire in her voice. "Even if that's true, how's that supposed to help me? I can't exactly walk up to some corporate bigwig and tell them a sob story about my daddy's medical bills."

"No, but you can create buzz. Generate interest. Make yourself someone they want to associate with." She resumes pacing. "The rodeo world is all about image, Clay. You need to give them something to talk about."

"Like what?"

She stops in front of me, setting her hands on her hips. "Sex appeal, Clay. That's your secret weapon. Sponsors will clamor to throw money at a rugged cowboy with the heart of a champion." Jo's eyes narrow on me, her gaze lingering on my face in a way that makes my skin itch. "You've got the looks, the talent, and the backstory. What you're missing is visibility."

I snort, shifting uncomfortably under her scrutiny. "Visibility? I'm competing in the same events as everyone else."

"And then disappearing to lick your wounds in private afterward." She gestures around the empty area behind the pens. "Meanwhile, Sterling's working the crowd, posing for photos, and making sure his face is plastered across every rodeo magazine and social media site."

"That's not my style," I mumble, but a nagging voice in my head wonders if she might be right.

"Your style is about to cost you your family ranch." Jo's words hit me like a slap to the face, sharp and stinging. "You think your pride is worth more than four generations of McKendrick blood, sweat, and tears?"

I jump up fast enough to make her take a step back. "Don't you dare—"

"What? Tell you the truth?" She doesn't back down, stepping closer instead until I can see the gold flecks in her green eyes. "Do you want to save that ranch or not, Clay? Because sitting here wallowing in self-pity sure as hell isn't gonna do it."

The anger builds in my chest, hot and fierce. Who the hell does she think she is? "You don't know a damn thing about what I'm willing to sacrifice for my family."

"Then prove it." Her voice drops to a near whisper. "Stop being so precious about your image and start playing the game like everyone else. Leverage that hot body."

The words hang in the air between us like smoke from a campfire, and heat flushes my face. Did Jo Callahan just call me hot? My brain scrambles to process that fact while my body responds in ways that are definitely not appropriate for a public conversation.

"My what now?" I manage to croak.

She rolls her eyes, but a faint pinkness creeps up her neck. "Don't let it go to your head, McKendrick. I'm talking strategy, not giving you a personal assessment."

"Right. Strategy." I clear my throat, trying to ignore the way my pulse has kicked up another notch. "And what exactly does this strategy involve?"

She smirks. "Come with me now, and you'll see."

Chapter Five

Learning the Ropes

Jolene Callahan drags me into her pickup truck and drives me to a location on the other side of Durango, parking in a gravel lot in front of a weathered, brightly lit building. As we exit the truck, I quickly realize what sort of place this is.

"A honky-tonk?" I say, grimacing at the gaudy decor. I can hear the country music blasting inside the building. "I'm starving, but I'd prefer someplace less…raucous."

Just as we mount the porch steps, Jo halts and swivels partway toward me, waggling one finger. "Now, now, Clay, don't be a stick in the mud. You need some serious relaxation, and your personal rodeo doctor has prescribed a night of honky-tonk therapy."

Her wicked grin makes me feel as if she's luring me into debauchery. Jo is the cutest, sexiest devil. I won't mind letting her corrupt me.

Jo bumps her hip into me. "Thought you wanted to learn about visibility. This is where your lesson begins."

Before I can protest, she pushes through the swinging doors. A wall of sound slams into me like a freight train. The Dusty Boot Bar is exactly what you'd expect from a roadhouse on the outskirts of nowhere—sawdust on the floor, neon beer signs flickering on wood-paneled walls, and a mechanical bull that's seen better decades. The air is thick with cigarette smoke, and the smell of fried food makes my stomach growl despite my reservations.

"Two beers," Jo hollers to the bartender, sliding onto a stool like she owns the place. Heads turn to follow her every movement.

I settle onto the stool beside her, acutely aware of how every conversation in our immediate vicinity has dropped to a whisper. Great. Just what I need—an audience.

"Relax," Jo whispers, nudging my shoulder with her own. "You look like you're about to bolt."

"Can you blame me?" I accept the beer from the bartender, a grizzled man with arms like tree trunks who's clearly been working this joint since the Carter administration. "Half the people in here are staring at us."

"Good." She takes a long pull from her bottle, scanning the room. Her gaze has the calculating precision of a general surveying a battlefield. "That's the whole point of this exercise."

"In what way? I'm confused, Jo. An explanation would be helpful."

Before she can respond to my query, a familiar voice calls out through the ruckus behind us. "Well, I'll be damned. If it isn't the second-place cowboy himself."

I don't need to turn around to know the jerk who's speaking is Brock Sterling. My jaw tightens as I sense his presence behind me, and the smell of his expensive cologne wafts through the room. His smugness is almost as pungent.

"Sterling," I acknowledge without glancing at him, and I deliberately swallow a large swig of my beer.

"And there's the beautiful Jo Callahan." Brock slides up to the bar beside me, close enough that his shoulder brushes mine. Territorial bastard. "Didn't expect to see rodeo royalty in a dive like this."

Jo doesn't even glance at Brock as she speaks. "Sometimes you need to get your hands dirty to remember where you came from, don't you think?"

"Can't say I relate." Brock signals the bartender for a whiskey, neat. "Some of us never forgot we belonged at the top."

The dig lands exactly where he intended, and my knuckles whiten around the beer bottle. Jo must sense my tension because her hand suddenly lands on my thigh, squeezing gently in what appears to be a warning.

"Clay and I were just celebrating his impressive performance to-day," she declares, her voice carrying far enough to draw attention from nearby tables. "Two-tenths of a second behind you, Brock."

Brock's smile falters for a fraction of a second before he recovers. "Impressive for a small-time rancher, I suppose. But we both know consistency is what separates the champions from the also-rans."

I open my mouth to fire back, but Jo digs her fingers deeper into my thigh. Her other hand slides up my arm, coming to rest against my biceps in a gesture that's unmistakably possessive.

"Clay has plenty of consistency," she proclaims.

Something shifts in Brock's expression, his eyes darting between Jo's face and her hand on my arm. I can practically hear the wheels turning in her mind.

"Your companion?" he repeats, his voice laced with disbelief. "Since when did you two become so…friendly?"

Jo leans in, gazing up at me like we're going steady. "Some things happen when you aren't looking, Sterling."

What the hell is she playing at?

Brock's gaze narrows, and his lips pucker faintly. "Last I heard, Jo wasn't exactly in the market for a cowboy. In fact, I heard she prefers…a different sort of companionship."

I clench my jaw so hard it hurts. If Brock doesn't shut his mouth, I might do it for him. But before I can respond, Jo grips my hand under the table, squeezing firmly. I get the point. She's urging me not to let Brock crawl under my skin.

I relax my posture, draping an arm around Jo's shoulders as I turn my focus to her. "Ready to boogie, darlin'?"

"Absolutely." Jo slides off her barstool with fluid grace. She twines her fingers with mine, and the contact sends an unexpected jolt through me. "I love this song."

I don't recognize whatever's blasting from the speakers, but I'm not about to admit that with Brock Sterling watching our every move. Jo tugs me toward the small dance floor where a handful of couples are swaying to the music. I follow because, hell, what else am I gonna do?

"I don't dance," I mutter close to her ear as we reach the edge of the wooden floor.

"Tonight, you will, Clay." She slides her hands up my chest and onto my shoulders. "Trust me, McKendrick. This is all part of the plan."

"Shouldn't your cohort be clued in?"

Jo ignores my question, already moving to the music. She sways those hips in a sensual rhythm that makes my mouth go dry and my brain forget how to form complete thoughts.

I squint my eyes, hoping to get her attention. "Are you still talking about that blasted 'visibility' hogwash?"

"Yes," she hisses through her teeth. "Half the rodeo circuit is in this bar tonight, and they're all watching us right now. Time to get the train rolling."

I glance around and realize she's right. Cowboys I recognize from earlier today are nursing beers at various tables, their eyes tracking our every movement. Even some of the buckle bunnies who usually orbit Sterling's crew are whispering behind their hands, pointing in our direction.

"So, we're putting on a show." I rest my hands on her waist because it seems like the natural place to put them.

"We're crafting a narrative, that's all." Her fingers toy with the hair at the base of my neck, sending shivers down my spine that have nothing to do with the air conditioning. "Clay McKendrick isn't just a struggling rancher anymore. He's the cowboy who caught the attention of Jo Callahan—rodeo royalty."

The sultry tone of her voice has me breathing a little harder. When she leans in closer, her lips graze my ear, and she whispers, "We're using each other to get what we both want." Her breath ghosts over my skin, warm and tempting.

Damn, I need to fuck Jo. But I've never been the type to use and discard a woman—or to let a woman do that to me. Before I take her back to the truck to screw her on the bench seat, I need to show her all my moves, the ones she's never seen before.

I brush my lips over the shell of her ear, making her shiver faintly. "Time to show you my best moves, Jolene Callahan."

Her brows lift, but she doesn't move a muscle.

So, I slide out of the booth and offer her my hand. "Are you tough enough to keep up with me on the dance floor?"

She holds out her hand to me, palm up, letting me pull her to her feet. "Oh please, I've been burning up the dance floor since I was eight years old."

The joint is packed tighter than sardines in a can, but Jo weaves through the crowd like she's done this a hundred times. I follow, hyperaware of every eye tracking our movement, every whispered conversation that stops when we pass by. The song shifts to a softer, more intimate ballad as Jo faces me and assumes the usual pose for slow dancing. She fits in my arms perfectly. As I settle my hands on her waist, she brushes her thumbs along the strip of skin where her shirt has ridden up slightly.

"You're thinking too hard again," she whispers, toying with the collar of my shirt. "Just move with me. It's not hard to do once you relax into it."

The music seems to wrap around us as if our bodies have merged, and I let myself get lost in the sensual rhythm. Jo's right. I am overthinking this. She initiates a leisurely pace while her hips move with mine and my hands sink lower to rest just above the curve of her ass. The moment feels right, as if we've always been meant to join our bodies this way. I need to kiss her so badly, need it like a starved man craves a meal after weeks in the desert with no food.

But then the ballad fades away, and a raucous number starts up as new couples take the floor. This is just what I need right now to distract myself from the feel of Jo's body molded to mine.

I wink at her. "Now the fun really begins."

Chapter Six

Blowing Off Steam

What could be better than a round of line dancing accompanied by upbeat country music? It's a cowboy tradition. I'm still holding Jo's hand, and I can't help smiling when I realize which dance we're starting with. It's the good ol' Tush Push. This dance is a longtime favorite of mine, and I smile even more when the music starts up. It's Billy Ray Cyrus singing "Achy Breaky Heart." Some people don't like that song, thinking it's too cheesy. But it's the perfect accompaniment to the Tush Push.

"Tush Push? Really?" Jo's eyes light up with recognition as the familiar beats fill the air. She grins and laughs, weaving through the crowd to find us a good spot. "I never would've pegged you for a line dancing fan."

"What's wrong, Callahan? Can't keep up?" I tease, knowing full well that she can probably dance circles around me.

"Just watch me, cowboy."

We stomp and slide in perfect sync with the crowd, our boots scuffing on the worn wooden floor. Jo moves her body with effortless precision and grace, every step executed with the same confidence she displays in the arena. I catch myself watching her more than I'm paying attention to my own steps.

"Eyes forward, McKendrick," she reminds me when she notices I'm staring at her ass. But a playful smile tugs at her lips.

The song ends, transitioning to another line dancing favorite of mine—the Boot Scootin' Boogie. Jo gets even more into it now, and the way her body moves, especially how her ass moves, makes it hard to keep my eye on the other dancers. I bump into somebody. Thankfully, everyone's having too much fun to care.

When we pivot on our heels, and our gazes lock, sizzling heat sparks between us. I know she feels it too, based on the look in her eye. The crowd on the dance floor seems to fade away, and suddenly, it's only the two of us kicking up our heels and bumping into each other on purpose. I never used to think line dancing was erotic. But damn, with Jo Callahan it is. The other dancers, the music, the heat of bodies crammed into a small space…it all vanishes from my awareness.

Then the music shifts. It transitions to a romantic ballad that has steamy undertones. Jo doesn't miss a beat. She wraps her arms around my neck and molds our bodies to each other, eliminating the space between us.

"Is this part of your visibility plan too?" I ask, my voice huskier than I intended.

"Maybe." Her gaze remains bound to mine. "Or maybe I just want to feel how solid you are."

She grinds her hips against me, making my cock jerk. The scent of her elicits a rush of blood heading south, and I know she can feel exactly what she's doing to me.

"Careful, Callahan," I warn. "This is starting to feel less like strategy and more like…seduction."

"Maybe it's both."

"Both, huh? That could get complicated."

She drags her tongue over her lips, deliberately teasing me. "Aren't you dying to kiss me, Clay? Strictly to find out how it would feel."

The sultry tone of her voice, coupled with the fluid way she moves that body, makes it hard for me to think. Jo's body is all fluid grace and barely contained fire, like a volcano about to erupt. Before I can answer her question, I sense a pair of eyes boring into my back. Turning slightly, I catch Brock Sterling watching us from the bar with his fists clenched and his eyes narrowed. Several phones are pointed in our direction, capturing what must look like quite the romantic moment.

"We've got an audience," I say quietly.

Jo follows my gaze and smirks. "Let them watch. Let Brock watch, I don't care. Do you?"

She presses her body closer, molding her curves against me in a way that makes every coherent thought scatter. The music thrums through the floorboards and up into my bones, but all I can focus on is the weight of her in my arms and the fluttering of her pulse beneath the delicate skin of her throat. When she tilts her head back to look up at me, the intensity in those emerald eyes makes my dick twitch. The song winds down, but neither of us tries to step away.

I thread my fingers between Jo's, guiding her away from the dance floor and the crowd. She stays quiet, licking her lips and smiling up at me with molten heat in her eyes. She wants me as much as I want her, that much is obvious. Maybe I shouldn't fuck her, but I can't resist seducing the rodeo queen. The way she weaves around barrels… It's poetry and sex all in one package. I haven't been with a woman in longer than I care to admit. The ranch, my PRCA dreams, they've consumed all of my time.

Now it's my turn to blow off some steam.

As I usher Jo over to her truck, I halt with one hand on the door. "I think you know what I want, Jolene."

She bites her bottom lip, releasing it little by little. "I want the same thing, Clay. Think you can make me come like a rocket ship flying to the moon?"

"Hell yeah."

I back her up against the side of the truck. I bracket her face with both hands as I capture her mouth with mine. She tastes like beer and something uniquely her, and when she parts her lips with a soft moan, I deepen the kiss until we're both breathing hard, tongues tangling in fervid exploration.

"Get in the truck," I growl.

Jo fumbles for the door handle behind her, and we tumble into the cab together. I lift her onto my lap while she frantically works at my belt buckle. I bury my face against her neck, dragging my tongue over her salty skin. Damn, even that part of her tastes like heaven.

"God, Clay," she moans while unfastening my jeans. "You're the hottest cowboy on the circuit, and I've been dying to get you between my legs."

"Shit, Jo, I'm so hard I might explode inside my briefs."

The only sound she makes is a soft "unh" that's rife with urgency.

I tug her shirt over her head, revealing a lacy black bra that's virtually transparent. Her tits almost spill over the cups, and I can't wait to feel those mounds in my hands. I need to taste them right now.

"Fuck, you're gorgeous," I snarl, brushing my thumbs over the lace-covered peaks. She arches into my touch, her head falling back against the seat.

Jo undoes the rivet on my jeans, rising to a crouch so she can yank my briefs and jeans down far enough to free my cock. My clothes are now trapped near my knees. I'm fully hard and raring to go, so pent up that I might erupt any second. But first, I need to get rid of her bra so I can devour those luscious nipples.

I reach behind her and unhook the clasp with practiced ease, sliding the straps down her shoulders until the lace falls away completely. Her breasts are even more perfect than I imagined—full and firm with rosy peaks that beg for me to gorge myself on their flavor.

"Christ, Jo," I rasp, cupping her tits roughly in my palms, flicking my thumbnails over the tips of her nipples Jo releases whimpering cry filled with desperation. "You're gonna be the death of me, sweet Jolene."

"Shut up and make me come." she gasps, her fingers frantically working at my shirt buttons. "Please hurry, Clay, please. I need to feel your skin on mine and dick inside me."

I help her push my shirt off my shoulders while she splays her hands over my chest, her nails scraping lightly over my skin. The sensation fires a heat-seeking missile straight into my cock. Reflexively, I groan low in my throat. "Shit, Jo, what are you doin' to me?"

She clasps my dick with both hands, grinding her folds into me again and again until her cream is dribbling onto the seat and her juices have drenched my cock. The aroma of her desire suffuses the cab, ramping up my lust even further.

"Damn, Jo, I need to fuck you so bad I'm going crazy," I groan, my hands gripping her hips as she rocks against me. "You're already so wet for me. I can smell it and almost taste it."

"I've been soaked ever since we started dancing," she pants, her breath hot against my ear. "Stop talking and fuck me, Clay."

A terrible thought suddenly hits me. "Oh, no. I don't have a condom."

"Don't worry, I've got one."

She reaches into her back pocket and pulls out a foil packet. When she rips the packet open with her teeth, I hiss in a breath. A bead of liquid lies poised on the head of my cock, and I know I can't wait much longer. But when she moves to sheath me herself, I grab her wrist to stop her.

"Sorry, darlin'. I'd better do that myself, or this'll be over before it starts."

The dim light inside the cab makes it more difficult to see her expression, though the neon sign on the honky-tonk provides a bit more illumination. Once I've got the condom on, Jo takes over again, sinking onto my dick so slowly that my pulse pounds in my ears. Damn, it feels amazing to have her wrapped around me, and I want to thrust up into her with every ounce of my strength. But I hold back, gritting my teeth as she adjusts to my size.

"Oh my God," Jo gasps, her head falling forward to rest on mine. Her inner walls clench around me in pulsating waves, hot and tight and perfect. "Can't believe how incredible this feels, Clay."

"Neither can I, darlin'." My voice is strained from the effort of staying still. "You're so tight, Jo, I—"

She rolls her hips against me in a fluid rocking motion, and whatever I meant to say dissolves into a long groan. Jo sets a rhythm that's almost torturous—slow and deliberate at first, then quickening the pace as her need to come escalates. My dick has never been this hard before. Jolene Callahan turns me on like nobody else ever could. I try to focus on Jo while she fucks me, but I get distracted by her breasts and the way they bounce with every movement. I can't resist leaning forward to corral one stiff peak between my lips.

"Oh, yes, Clay, yes-yes-yes!" she cries out, her fingers tangled in my hair while she clutches my head to her breast. The taste of her skin, salty and sweet, makes me growl against her nipple. I suck harder, using my teeth to graze the sensitive flesh, and she cries out softly.

"That's it, baby," I mumble against her breast before switching to the other one briefly. "Let me hear you say my name, darlin', please."

Jo's movements grow more urgent as she grinds her hips down over and over, riding me with increasing desperation. Little grunts tumble from her lips. The truck rocks with our movements while the windows begin to fog up from the heat we're generating with our bodies. I grip her ass, helping to guide her rhythm as she takes what she needs from me.

I don't know how much longer I can hold out.

"Clay, I'm so close," she whimpers as her nails dig into my shoulders. "Don't stop, please don't stop."

I thrust up to meet her downward strokes, the angle hitting that perfect spot inside her that makes her gasp and arch her back. Her inner muscles flutter around me, and I can tell she's climbing toward the edge of a cliff.

"That's it, Jo," I snarl. "Come for me, darlin', do it *right now.*"

Her rhythm falters as the pleasure escalates and her breaths turn into ragged gasps against my neck. I can feel the tension coiling in her body, every muscle drawn tight as she chases her release.

I need to let go too, but not until she does. My cock is stiff as a board, but I can feel the sizzling power of my release rolling down my spine. That means I don't have much time. So, I swallow one nipple and suck so hard so fast that she can't hold out anymore.

"Clay, I'm—oh God—I'm about to—"

Her words dissolve into a scream of pure ecstasy as she blows apart in my arms. Her body convulses around my cock in waves of pleasure so intense that I can't hold back my own climax for much longer. The way she shouts my name, broken and breathless, almost undoes me completely.

And I give up on holding out. "Jo, baby, keep fucking me until I'm spent."

She does exactly that, pumping her hips harder and faster while I shout and release everything I have inside her sweet little body. My shout of ecstasy is almost deafening inside the truck. After a couple more spasms, my dick is done—and I'm spent too.

I'm speechless from what we just did. So, all I can do is hold onto her hips and watch while she rides out the aftershocks. "You're amazing."

"You're not so bad yourself, cowboy," she whispers, her voice deliciously raspy.

I touch my forehead to hers, both of us panting as we come down from our shared high. Sex has never been this mind-blowing for me, not ever. Jolene Callahan does this to me.

We stay this way for a while, our bodies still joined, our breath mingling. The windows are completely fogged up now, creating a private cocoon around us. Jo's skin seems to glow with a thin sheen of sweat, and I can't resist gliding my hands up her sides, marveling at how soft she feels beneath my calloused palms.

Then she climbs off my lap and wrestles with her clothes until she's presentable for public viewing again. Jo waves toward the driver's door, where I'm still sitting. "Thanks for the awesome sex, Clay. I really needed it. Here's twenty bucks. It should cover cab fare back to wherever you left your pickup."

When she tries to shoo me away, I grasp her upper arms to stall her exit. "Jolene Callahan, are you trying to twist this into a one-time quickie? 'Cause that's total bullshit."

"I have no interest in relationships. Everybody knows that."

"Jo—"

When I don't move, she scrambles over me and pushes the door open, slithering out of the cab like a thief trying to escape from the cops. Except this is her truck. Why is she running away? Guess she's as confused as I am.

I lean halfway out the door and shout, "Where are you going, Jo? This is your truck."

She freezes for a moment, then gradually rotates toward me. And she makes a sheepish face. "Yeah, I forgot it's my truck."

I shake my head in disbelief, climbing out of the truck to halt beside her. "Come on, Jo, let's talk about this."

She chews on the inside of her lip for a moment. Then she waves for me to go away. "See you at the next rodeo, McKendrick."

Jo hurries back to her vehicle.

I'm so damn confused I can't think straight. By the time I've regained my senses, her truck is racing down the road amid a storm of dust.

On the cab ride back to my place, all I can think about is Jolene Callahan and the look on her face when she came all over my cock.

Chapter Seven

Spotlight Rodeo

The Texas heat feels like a living thing pressing against my skin. Two months have gone by since I last saw Jolene Callahan in the flesh—or even on a TV screen. After our mind-blowing sex in her pickup truck, she threw me away like a discarded takeout box. Whatever her problem is, I don't give a hoot anymore. My career as a professional rodeo cowboy takes precedence over just about everything else.

That includes Jo Callahan.

Fortunately, there's no rodeo today. I've arrived a few days early because…No, it has nothing to do with a certain sexy barrel racer. Like I said, my career as a professional rodeo cowboy matters more than anything else these days. My stats have improved enough that I'm actually making decent money now—not championship-level money, but enough to keep the ranch afloat for a while and make sure Dad's medical bills remain under control. That's what matters.

This isn't my first time performing at a Texas rodeo, but it is my debut at Frontier Days in Weatherford, the seat of Parker County. I hear there'll be a big kickoff in a few days featuring a cattle drive, a parade, and a street dance. Now that's what I need after so long on the road.

I adjust my hat and survey the rodeo grounds which are already bustling with activity this morning. Everybody wants to get an early start to adjust to the new environment. The familiar scent of hay, leather, and livestock fills my senses and centers me in a way nothing else can. This is my world, and I've earned my place in it with blood, sweat, and sheer determination.

"Clay McKendrick, you son of a gun!"

Buck's voice booms across the grounds, and I grin as I turn to see him striding toward me. The man looks the same as ever—weathered face, silver belt buckle catching the morning sun, and that infectious energy that makes everyone around him feel like they're about to witness something extraordinary.

"Buck, you crafty old coot!" I shout, grinning as I jog across the distance between us with long strides. "Didn't expect to see you here. Thought you were calling Cheyenne this week."

"Switched up my schedule at the last minute." He clasps my shoulder with a firm grip. "Couldn't miss seeing my favorite up-and-comer take on Weatherford. It's an iconic site for rodeo, and some famous cowboys have made their names here. Besides, the sponsors requested me specifically." He winks, tapping the side of his nose. "Seems someone's been generating quite the buzz lately."

I bow my head and clear my throat. Ever since that night with Jo, something bizarre has been happening. Photos of us dancing appeared on social media, and suddenly people were gossiping about Clay McKendrick—the Montana cowboy who caught the eye of rodeo royalty. Sponsors had started reaching out, and my performance numbers had climbed steadily.

I guess Jo was right about exposure after all.

"Just focusing on my upcoming events," I reply to Buck.

But we both know it's more than that. Buck is a smart man. The visibility strategy Jo had laid out before the pickup truck sex incident has been working better than I ever imagined. "Hey Buck, who else is competing this weekend?"

His expression shifts slightly, and I catch something in his eyes that makes my mouth go dry. "Well now, interesting you should ask. Got quite the lineup this time around. Sterling's here, of course, along with most of the usual suspects." He pauses, studying my face. "And word is Jo Callahan's making an appearance too."

My throat constricts, but I keep my expression neutral. "That so?"

"Yep. Heard she's been having quite the season herself. Three first-place finishes in the last month alone." Buck's wrinkles crease into what might be concern or humor—with him, it's hard to tell. "Are you two still...?"

"Still what?" I cut him off, a bit too hastily. "There was never any 'us,' Buck. Just a couple of drinks and some dancing."

Yeah, I'm leaving out the scorching sex in Jo's truck. Nobody needs to hear about that.

Buck raises an eyebrow but knows better than to pester me. Smart man. The truth is, I've been struggling to forget about that night for two months now, and I'm not about to dissect it with Buck in the middle of the rodeo grounds where anyone might overhear.

"Right, nothing at all between you and Jo," the old man says, drawing out the word as if it sounds odd to his ears. "Well, anyway, she's scheduled to compete Saturday evening. Barrel racing finals." He adjusts his hat, squinting at me in the subdued morning light. "Might want to prepare yourself, son. This circuit's smaller than you think and avoiding someone gets mighty difficult when you're both chasing prize money."

I grunt and return my attention to unloading Thunder from the trailer. The gelding snorts as I lead him down the ramp, eager to stretch his legs after the long drive.

"Not avoiding anyone," I mutter, more to myself than to Buck. "No time for women or gossip or...whatever."

"Mm-hm." Buck's knowing hum grates on my nerves. "Well, while you're avoiding the ladies, you might want to know the PRCA brass will be watching this weekend. Word is they're looking for fresh faces for their promotional materials next season."

That gets my attention. "Promotional materials?"

"Posters, commercials, maybe even some of those fancy social media campaigns the kids are all about these days." Buck rocks back on his heels, seeming entirely too pleased with himself. "Jo Callahan had a good idea, son. Her plan must've rubbed off on you. People are talking about Clay McKendrick these days."

I busy myself with checking Thunder's legs, trying not to let Buck see how his words have affected me. Promotional materials for the PRCA would mean serious money—the kind that could keep the ranch secure for years, not just months. "That's, uh...good to know, Buck. I'll be sure to bring my A-game."

"You'll need more than that, kid." He lowers his voice to a near whisper. "They're looking for the complete package. Someone with skill, sure, but also someone with star quality. Someone the fans connect with."

I straighten up, fixing him with a hard stare. "What exactly are you trying to say?"

He holds my gaze, unflinching. "I'm suggesting that whatever happened between you and Jo Callahan caught people's attention in a way that your riding alone never did. Chemistry like that doesn't come along every day."

"There is no chemistry," I snap, then immediately regret my tone when Buck's eyebrows shoot up.

"Whoa there, son. Guess I hit a nerve, hey?" He holds up his hands in surrender, but the knowing gleam in his eyes is unmistakable. "All I'm saying is opportunity doesn't knock twice. Sometimes you gotta open the door even if you're not sure what's on the other side."

I turn back to Thunder, running my hand along his neck to calm myself as much as him. "Sorry. It's been a long drive."

"Always is." Buck checks his watch and sighs. "Gotta run. I have a meeting with the event coordinator in ten. But listen, there's a little get-together at The Rusty Spur tonight. Sponsors, competitors, the whole rodeo family. Might be worth showing your face."

"Uh-huh. I'll think about it."

Buck gazes at something past my shoulder, then winks at me. "Have fun, kid."

Then he saunters away.

And I whirl around to see…Jolene Callahan. I probably look like a cartoon character with my eyes almost popping out of my head and my mouth hanging open far enough to let a squirrel crawl in there. I'd figured Jo might turn up at the Parker County rodeo event. But somehow, I still wasn't prepared for seeing her again.

Jo sashays up to me. "Hello, Clay, how've you been?"

"Uh, good. How about you?" What a dumbass conversation we're having. "Will you be competing in the barrel racing event?"

"You bet I will," she declares, adjusting her hat so it shields her eyes from the Texas sun. "Been on a winning streak lately. Three firsts in the last month."

I nod, trying to act like I didn't already know that. Like I haven't been tracking her results in every rodeo publication I can get my hands on.

"Congrats." I avoid glancing at her, instead fussing with Thunder's lead rope in my hands. "I'm happy for you, Jo."

She ambles toward me, and the familiar scent of her wafts in the air, sensual and sweet. "Clay, about that night in Durango—"

"Water under the bridge," I cut her off, not wanting to rehash how she tossed me out of her truck with cab fare like I was some cheap hookup. "We both got what we needed."

She bites her lip, and something almost like hurt flickers over her features before her trademark mask slides back into place. "Right. Of course." She adjusts her hat again, a nervous tell I remember. "I just wanted to make sure there wouldn't be any awkwardness between us."

"Nope, it's all good." *You big fat liar, Clay.* I can practically feel devil horns sprouting on my head. "We're both professionals, Jo. It's all good."

"Glad to hear it." She nods curtly, but her eyes search my face. "Thing is, I heard the PRCA bigwigs are scouting this weekend. Wouldn't want any personal distractions to get in the way for either of us."

The way she says 'distractions' stings more than it probably should. Like what happened between us was nothing more than a momentary lapse in judgment.

"Nice to see you again, Jo," I blurt out while I lead Thunder toward the stables. "I'm here to ride, same as always."

I'm about to turn away when she catches up to me, walking alongside while we shuffle into the stable. "Hold up, Clay, please. I need to talk to you about something."

With a heavy sigh, I halt Thunder and rotate halfway toward Jo. "What is it?"

"I'm so sorry, Clay. I should never have kicked you to the curb that way back in Durango."

Chapter Eight

Unexpected Confessions

What is Jo up to now? She claims that she regrets the way she treated me in her truck that night outside the honky-tonk. Okay, great. She knows she screwed up. But I'm waiting for her to explain why she tossed me out like a bag of garbage. Right now, she's just staring at me while biting her lip. If she thinks pitiful puppy eyes will wear me down…Aw, hell, she's right about that. But she should be the one to apologize.

I fold my arms over my chest while still holding the lead rope. "Okay, what have you got to say, Miss Callahan?"

Jo shifts her weight from one boot to the other, her fingers fidgeting with the brim of her hat. For someone who can face down a passel of drunk cowboys without flinching, she sure looks nervous right now.

"I was scared," she finally admits, her voice barely above a whisper. "That night, what happened between us…it made me feel confused and off balance."

My heart does that annoying beat-skipping thing it always does when she's honest with me. "What exactly are you afraid of, Jo?"

"Feeling something again." The words tumble out like she's been holding them back for months. "After my divorce, I swore off getting involved with anyone on the circuit. Too complicated, too risky." She meets my gaze, and I sense unexpected vulnerability there. "But then I met a tall, handsome cowboy who made me feel things I didn't want to feel. So, I panicked and pushed you away. Hard."

She searches my face for a reaction, but I'm not giving her the satisfaction. Not yet. She has some serious groveling to do first.

"Well, congratulations on the successful evasive maneuver," I quip. "Mission accomplished, Miss Callahan."

"Clay…" She steps closer. "I've regretted it every day since."

Thunder shifts restlessly beside me, sensing the tension. I stroke his neck absently, buying myself time to process what she told me. "That's a nice speech, Jo. Did you rehearse it on the drive over?"

She flinches, as if I've slapped her, but recovers quickly. "I deserved that."

"Yeah, you did." I sigh, some of the anger draining out of me as I see the genuine remorse in her eyes and on her face. "Look, I get it. We all have our reasons for keeping walls up. But that doesn't excuse you treating me the way you did."

She removes her hat, lowering her head, and runs her fingers through her auburn hair. "I handled it all wrong. The truth is, that night scared the hell out of me because you made love to me like it meant something, like *I* meant something to you. And that terrified me more than any angry stallion I've ever faced."

Thunder nickers softly, and I realize I've been standing here longer than I intended. Other competitors are starting to filter into the stable area, and the last thing I need is more gossip about Jo and me.

"So, what do you want from me now?" I ask, genuinely curious. "Forgiveness? A do-over?"

"Not sure. Maybe I just want the chance to not screw it up this time."

I probe her expression, hunting for any sign she's playing me. But all I see is a woman who looks as confused and conflicted as I feel. "Jo, I—"

"Clay McKendrick, imagine seeing you again! Ready to get whupped again?"

Brock Sterling's voice cuts through our conversation like a rusty blade. He strides over with that trademark swagger, his sponsor patches gleaming in the stable lighting. Perfect timing, as always.

"Sterling," I acknowledge with a nod, stepping slightly in front of Jo.

"And the lovely Miss Callahan is here too." Brock tips his hat with exaggerated politeness. "Heard you two have been the talk of the circuit lately. Congratulations on your recent wins, Jo."

"Thanks," she replies, her professional mask sliding back into place so smoothly it's like watching an actress step into character. "You're looking well, Brock."

"Can't complain. Three straight wins will do that for a man." His smile is all teeth and no warmth as his gaze shifts between us. "Speaking of wins, I heard the PRCA scouts are particularly interested in partnerships this season. Marketing gold, they're calling it—the right cowboy and cowgirl duo for their new campaign."

I grit my teeth, trying not to let Brock goad me into snarling at him. Naturally, he would know about that before the rest of us. His daddy's connections run deeper than oil wells in this business.

"Guess you and Maddie will be getting his-and-hers facelifts then, huh?" Jo's voice remains perfectly level, but I note the slight tension in her shoulders. "Gotta look good for the cameras, right, Brock?"

Brock rolls his eyes. "Oh please. My face is picture perfect."

I glance up at the sky briefly, shaking my head. "Uh-huh, Brock, whatever you say."

"Big money's on the line, McKendrick. Seven figures for the right pair." Brock's eyes glitter with a visible appetite for fame and glory that makes my lip curl. "Course, they're looking for authenticity. Real chemistry. Like the kind you and I could have, Jo. Imagine the possibilities, babe. Two champions, both at the top of our games and sexy as hell."

The way he says it, like I'm not standing right here, makes my blood simmer. But before I can say anything, Jo steps forward, her chin lifting in that defiant way that always makes me want to kiss her until she melts in my arms.

Jo hooks her thumbs in the waistband of her jeans. "Funny thing about chemistry, Brock. It isn't something you can manufacture in a boardroom."

Sterling's smile falters for half a second before he recovers. "Maybe you're right about chemistry, but it helps when both parties are actually winners. Consistent winners." His gaze flicks to me dismissively. "Some of us can't afford to hitch our wagons to shooting stars that might burn out."

That does it. I hand Thunder's lead rope to Jo without a word and stomp toward Sterling, coming near enough that I can see the uncertainty in his cold blue eyes. "Know what's funny? Last I checked, I was ranked fourth in the standings. That's hardly burning out."

"Fourth place is first loser, McKendrick." Sterling's voice carries just loud enough for the other competitors filtering into the stable to hear. "But hey, I'm sure your little ranch appreciates the participation trophies."

The mention of my ranch hits exactly where he intended, and my hands clench into fists. Jo's sharp intake of breath reminds me where we are, who's watching, and what's at stake.

"Easy, cowboy," Jo whispers under her breath, her hand grazing my arm. The contact grounds me, pulling me back from doing something stupid that would give Sterling exactly what he wants.

Brock smirks. "Jo, you're a smart girl. You know which side your bread's buttered on. Ain't that right, Jo-Jo? Me, I've got all the butter any girl could hope for."

"Then you find one of those girls. I'm taken."

Brock's brows hike up, and he seems genuinely baffled. "That's bullshit. Everybody knows you prefer horses over cowboys."

Not sure what he's implying, but it makes me want to march over there and punch him in the jaw hard enough to break it. Though I'd love to see Sterling with his jaw wired shut, eating through a straw, I won't give him the satisfaction.

I stick to that promise until he opens his mouth again.

Sterling grins and winks at Jo, cupping his groin with one hand. "Come on, sweet thing. Let a real man show you how it's done."

I fist my hands, seething like I've done before. "Brock, you slimy son of a bitch—"

Jo slings an arm around my waist, tugging me close. "Like I told you, Sterling, I'm taken. Clay and I have been seeing each other quietly for months. In fact, we're engaged."

What in tarnation is she talking about? Engaged? That's news to me, but I won't let on to Brock that I'm confused. All I can do is play along and hope she'll explain later. So, I sling my arm around her shoulders as I smile down at Jo while I inform Sterling, "That's right. We've kept it on the down-low until we were ready to announce the engagement. Now seems like as good a time as any. Jo's my sweet little dumpling."

Jo jabs me in the side, and I realize I might've laid it on a bit thick with the "sweet little dumpling" comment. But Brock's expression is worth the pain. His perfect smile freezes, then cracks at the edges.

"Engaged," he repeats flatly. "You expect me to believe that?"

Jo's diamond sharp smile doesn't waver. "Believe what you want, Sterling. We weren't planning to make it public until after Nationals, but"—She gazes up at me with an expression so tender it almost convinces me—"some things are worth celebrating early."

Thunder snorts and paws the ground, as if even he can sense the bullshit in the air. I stroke his neck to calm him while maintaining my poker face.

"Where's the ring?" Sterling challenges, his gaze narrowing as he glances at Jo's naked left hand.

"It's getting resized," she explains smoothly, wiggling her ring finger. "Clay's got these big ole hands, and he overestimated my size when he picked it out. Isn't that right, honey?"

The endearment rolls off her tongue like she's been saying it for years, and I find myself nodding along with her story. "Guilty as charged. Figured it was better to go too big than too small."

Sterling's jaw ticks, his composure finally beginning to crack. "How convenient."

"Isn't it?" Jo threads her fingers with mine. "We should probably get going, babe. Thunder needs settling in, and I promised I'd help you practice your new technique."

My new technique? I don't have a clue what she's talking about. Fortunately, I don't need to spout more lies to Brock. He shakes his head, clearly baffled, then strides away.

I bow my head, hissing words out under my breath. "Now we're engaged? You're insane, Jo."

"Maybe. But there is an upside to my lie." She raises onto her tiptoes to whisper into my ear, "Now everyone will be talking about us and not Brock Sterling."

I grin. "Jolene Callahan, you are a genius."

Chapter Nine

Rivals and Revelations

As I stand at the edge of the arena here in Weatherford, my gaze keeps returning to a certain barrel racer with mesmerizing green eyes who has become my fake fiancée. How did that happen? I think Jo is a sexy witch drawing me into her magical web, convincing me to do whatever she wants. But right now, she's about to take her turn at the barrels. I'm waiting with bated breath to see her performance. As usual, Buck is narrating the whole rodeo—starting with Jo and the other ladies. I know from experience they're tough competitors.

A few days ago, Jo and I, as well as plenty of other folks, watched the Cattle Drive through town. Afterward, the Frontier Days festivities kicked into high gear with a parade and a street dance. We kicked our heels up for every line dance plus old traditional favorites. That included the Tush Push, which had us both grinning like fools, remembering that night at the honky-tonk. Somehow, being Jo's fake fiancé feels both terrifying and right. The crowd thinks we're in love, and sometimes, when she looks at me a certain way, I almost believe it myself.

But tonight, the rodeo begins in earnest.

I also noticed Brock Sterling in the stands—with Maddie Vale, his occasional sidekick. She and Jo have a bit of a rivalry going on. My engagement to Jo, fake or not, deserves a real ring, so I bought her one yesterday. It's a simple, modest stone set in white gold. I don't think Jo was faking it when she declared it's the most beautiful ring ever.

Buck's voice booms through the speakers. "Next up, ladies and gentlemen, is our favorite barrel racer, the queen of the rodeo, Jolene Callahan!"

Jo bursts out of the gate, her body moving in perfect harmony with her horse, the determination on her face evident. There's something mesmerizing about watching her ride—the way she leans into the turns, her hair flying out behind her as her expression reveals her fierce concentration. Jolene Callahan is a vision of beauty, fluid grace, and raw power—a combination that makes me horny.

Damn, I need to kiss Jo. And do other things with her…

"Check out that form, folks!" Buck exclaims. "Callahan's on fire today!"

Jo rounds the first barrel, her body angled at just the perfect degree, the crowd roars its approval. I suddenly realize I'm gripping the railing hard enough that my knuckles turn white.

"Would you look at that time on the first turn!" Buck shouts. "Callahan's on pace to break her own record!"

I watch in rapt wonder as Jo thunders toward the second barrel. Her connection with that horse is incredible. They seem to share the same brain, the same heartbeat. The way she anticipates every movement, shifting her weight with subtle grace…You'd miss it if you weren't looking for it.

And I'm definitely looking.

Abruptly, some kind of noise echoes across the arena. Maddie's horse—tied nearby—rears up unexpectedly, spooking several animals near the gate. The commotion carries over to Jo's horse, who hesitates for a split second before rounding the final barrel. Even from this distance, I can tell Jo has tensed up slightly as she fights to maintain control. The crowd collectively holds its breath.

"Whoa there!" Buck calls out, his voice rife with confusion. But he recovers quickly. "Looks like we've got some unexpected excitement at the gate! "Callahan's fighting to keep her line!"

Jo leans over, petting her horse's neck, and whispers something to her mount that I can't hear. Well, I am way over at the opposite end of the arena. Whatever magic spell Jo whispered to her horse, it worked. The mare steadies and makes the turn, but it's wider than it should, meaning Jo lost precious seconds.

"Callahan recovers," Buck hollers, "but that's gonna cost her on the clock, folks!"

Buck continues his commentary, following along as Jo races toward the finish line. My heart pounds, the crowd falls silent, and I stop breathing while Jo dashes past the line. Now we all wait to hear the judges' decision.

The numbers flash on the board: 16.7 seconds. Good, but not great. Jo's face tells the whole story as she exits the arena. Disappointment flickers in those green eyes, but only for a split second. Then she pats her horse's neck, murmuring praise despite the less-than-perfect run.

I start moving before I consciously decide to, pushing through the crowd of competitors and spectators until I reach Jo. Then I kiss her cheek. "Hell of a recovery out there, and that's not bullshit. You were fantastic."

Jo looks up at me, then sighs. Her posture wilts. "Should've been faster. That spook cost me the win."

"Was it Maddie's horse?" I glance toward where Sterling's occasional companion is tending to her mount, acting like nothing happened.

"Could've been an accident. Horses can get spooked." Jo's tone that tells me she doesn't believe that for a second.

"Accident my ass," I grumble. Maddie's smug expression as she brushes her horse's mane proves to me that she spooked Jo's mare. "That woman's about as accidental as a rattlesnake in your boot."

Jo follows my gaze, her jaw tightening. "Maybe, but I can't prove anything. And making accusations without evidence would only make me look like a sore loser."

She's right, but it doesn't stop the protective urge that rises inside me. I've seen enough dirty tricks in the rodeo world to recognize one when I see it. Maddie's timing was too perfect—right as Jo approached that final barrel.

I rest my hand on the small of Jo's back. "You are no loser, darlin'. That recovery was something else. Most riders would've blown the whole run."

A ghost of a smile touches her lips. "When did you become a sweet talker, Clay?"

"I have my moments." Rising onto my tiptoes to survey the arena, I search for some explanation for what happened, but I see nothing. "Wait here, Jo. I'll be back in a minute."

While I jog over to Brock and Maddie, I suddenly realize Jo is right behind me. I slip my fingers between hers, and we march over there hand in hand. I'm hoping to avoid a serious confrontation. "Hey, did you guys hear a crunching-crackling sound right before Maddie's horse spooked?"

Brock's eyebrows shoot up in the phoniest innocent act I've ever seen. "Crunching sound? Can't say I heard anything unusual. Did you, Maddie?"

His cohort's smile is as sweet as antifreeze while she strokes her horse's neck. "Just the normal arena sounds. Maybe your hearing isn't so good, McKendrick. Or you might just be looking for excuses for your fiancée's mediocre performance."

Jo's fingers tighten around mine, and I feel her body tense beside me. But her voice remains cool when she speaks. "Mediocre or not, it's strange how your horse only spooked when I was on my final barrel. Quite the coincidence, hey?"

"Some horses are sensitive," Maddie shrugs, her blonde ponytail swinging. "Not everyone can afford championship bloodlines like yours, Jo."

I stride forward, ready to rain hell down on Brock and Maddie. But Jo's grip on my hand tightens, and I realize she wants to deal with her nemesis.

"You're absolutely right, Maddie," Jo says, her voice dripping with false sweetness. "Not everyone can afford quality breeding. Some people have to rely on cheap tricks instead of actual talent."

Maddie's sugary smile falters for a heartbeat, then she recovers. "I have no idea what you're implying, Callahan."

"Of course you don't." Jo puckers her lips, tilting her head, studying Maddie with the same intensity she brings to reading a horse's movements. "And you also had no idea your horse would spook at exactly the right moment to mess up my run."

I sling an arm around Jo's shoulders, urging her to turn around with me and walk away. She spears Maddie and Brock with a vicious scowl but keeps walking away. Whatever those two are up to, we don't have time to worry about it now.

The next competitor is already lining up at the gate. Jo and I retreat to the sidelines, both of us simmering with frustration.

"Those two are up to no good," I mutter, keeping my voice low as we find a spot along the fence.

"I know. But without proof, there's nothing we can do."

Across the arena, I spot Maddie and Brock huddling together. Maddie's hand slips into her jacket pocket, removing a small object that glints faintly in the arena lights before disappearing into Brock's waiting palm. The exchange is so quick I almost miss it.

"Did you see that?" I whisper, nudging Jo's shoulder.

"See what?"

"That hand-off. Maddie just passed something to Brock."

Jo veers her gaze straight toward Sterling as he makes his way toward the contestants' area where the bull riders are gathered. She wriggles out of my embrace, and I trot along beside her. We zigzag through the crowd as we try to keep Brock in sight without being obvious about it. He halts near the chutes, casually leaning against a fence post while chatting with one of the stock contractors. From our position behind an equipment trailer, we can just make out his profile.

"What do you think they're planning?" I ask, keeping my voice low.

Jo shakes her head. "Nothing good. They're passing something between them like they're in some spy movie."

"Maybe we should tell the officials."

"And say what? That we saw them hand off a suspicious package that we couldn't see clearly or identify? Without knowing what it was, we'd sound paranoid."

It's too late, anyway. Brock just retreated to the sidelines, and Maddie is about to take her turn.

Buck's voice drowns out all other sounds as Maddie prepares for her run. "Next up, we have Maddie Vale from Dallas, Texas!"

Jo's hand finds mine, her grip tight as we watch Maddie burst out of the gate. Her form is solid, I'll give her that. But sense calculation in the way she rides—like she's more focused on the clock than the connection with her horse.

"Sixteen-point-two seconds for Maddie Vale!" Buck announces as she crosses the finish line. "That puts her in second place behind Sarah Martinez!"

I feel Jo's shoulders relax a little. At least Maddie didn't win. But the smug expression on her face as she exits the arena tells me she's not disappointed. If anything, she seems satisfied, like everything is going according to plan.

"That's a decent time," Jo admits grudgingly. "Guess all I can do is shrug it off and move on."

But I will never forget what went down today. Never. Nobody messes with my girl.

Chapter Ten

Home on the Range

Jo trounced Maddie Vale in her last round of barrel racing, and I whooped and shouted like an idiot to support my girl. The sounds echo across the arena, drawing amused looks from nearby spectators, but I don't give a damn. Jo earned that victory fair and square, and after what Maddie pulled earlier, watching her get beat by a superior rider feels like justice served with a side of sweet revenge.

Jo grins as she exits the arena. Her cheeks are flushed with the pride of victory. Her eyes sparkle with the kind of satisfaction that comes from proving your worth when someone tries to tear you down.

"Fifteen-point-eight!" Buck shouts. "Ladies and gentlemen, that's a new arena record for Jolene Callahan!"

The crowd erupts, and I find myself hollering again, this time joined by half the stands. Jo raises her hand in acknowledgment, but her eyes find mine amid the chaos. The triumphant grin she aims at me is the sweetest thing I've ever seen.

But now, it's time for one of my best events.

"Ladies and gentlemen," Buck hollers through the PA, "it's time for a fan favorite event. Bull riding!"

The eight-second countdown that could make or break my weekend. I experience the familiar pre-ride nerves as I check my gear one final time. The bull rope feels solid in my hands, the rosin sticky against my palm.

"First up, Clay McKendrick from Montana, riding your favorite bull—Tornado Alley!"

I nod to the gate crew and settle onto the massive black beast's back. Tornado Alley shifts beneath me, two thousand pounds of muscle and bad attitude just waiting to launch me into orbit. I wrap the rope around my hand, testing the grip.

"You got this, cowboy!" Jo shouts through the crowd noise, and I glance up to see her pressed against the rail. That new arena record she achieved makes her glow from head to toe. The sight of her cheering for me…it shoots a jolt of determination through my veins that's stronger than any adrenaline rush.

I settle deeper into the rope, feeling Tornado's muscles bunch beneath me. The bull's reputation precedes him—he's sent more cowboys to the dirt than a bucking bronc convention, but that just makes the challenge sweeter.

"Ready?" the gate man calls out.

I nod once, sharp and decisive. "Turn him loose."

The gate swings open and Tornado Alley explodes out of the chute like a black hurricane. The first buck nearly rattles my teeth loose, but I clamp down with my legs and let my free arm find its rhythm. One Mississippi, two Mississippi…

The world becomes a blur of spinning dirt and sky as Tornado Alley twists his massive frame, trying every trick in his considerable playbook. A sharp right spin followed by a bone-jarring drop that would've unseated me six months ago. But I'm not the same rider I was back then. I've got more than ranch bills driving me now.

Five Mississippi, six Mississippi…

Tornado changes tactics, bucking straight up before slamming back down with enough force to make my spine compress. My vision blurs for a split second, but I recover, finding my center again as the crowd roars somewhere beyond the dust cloud we're kicking up.

Seven Mississippi…

One more second. Just one more. Tornado Alley twists violently beneath me, his massive head swinging around as if he's trying to find me, to knock me loose with those horns. I lean back, compensating for the movement, my free arm windmilling to keep my balance.

Eight Mississippi!

The buzzer sounds just as the bull executes a perfect spin that finally breaks my grip. I'm airborne for a heart-stopping second before I hit the dirt hard, rolling away from those lethal hooves as the bullfighters rush in to distract Tornado Alley. My lungs burn as dust fills my throat, but I'm scrambling to my feet with a grin splitting my face. I made it. I fucking made it! Eight seconds on one of the toughest bulls in the circuit.

"Ladies and gentlemen, Clay McKendrick stays on for the full eight seconds!" Buck's voice reverberates through the arena, and he seems almost more excited than I am. Even the crowd leaps to their feet. "Let's see those scores!"

I dust myself off, my heart still hammering in my chest as I look up at the scoreboard. The judges' numbers flash across the screen: 87.5. Not my best, but damn solid considering Tornado Alley's reputation.

"That's good enough to put McKendrick in first place!" Buck announces, and the throng erupts again.

I tip my hat to the crowd, but my eyes are searching for Jo. I find her jumping up and down by the rail, her face lit up with pure joy. She cups her hands around her mouth and shouts something I can't hear over the noise, but the way she's beaming makes my chest swell with pride.

"Not bad for a rancher boy," Brock Sterling's voice interrupts my celebration makes my jaw clench. He's leaning against the fence, arms crossed, that trademark smirk firmly in place. "Course, you still got to outlast the rest of us."

I resist the urge to tell him exactly where he can shove his commentary. Instead, I simply nod toward the chutes where the next rider is getting ready. "Guess we'll see about that, Sterling."

"Guess we will." His gaze narrows as he watches Jo wending her way toward us. "Funny how your scores have been improving ever since you started playing house with Queen Jolene over there. Makes a man wonder if you're getting some extra...coaching."

His caustic tone makes my blood boil. But before I can snarl an epithet at Brock, Jo appears at my side. She's still glowing from her own victory. When she slides her arm around my waist, I can't help smiling just like she is.

"Congratulations on the ride, honey," Jo says loud enough for Sterling to hear. Then she rises onto her tiptoes to press a quick kiss on my cheek.

"Thanks, darlin'," I reply, pulling her closer and relishing the way Sterling's jaw tightens. "Your turn to celebrate. That record's gonna be tough to beat."

"Speaking of beating things," Brock turns to face me directly. "Don't expect your scores today to be repeated. This was a fluke, McKendrick."

I shrug off his taunts. "How 'bout I buy you a beer, Brock? No hard feelings."

His nostrils flare just like the bull I rode a few minutes ago. But he says nothing. Only glares at me. After a few seconds, Brock stalks off in the other direction.

"You're the king of the cowboys, Clay McKendrick," Jo says loud enough for Sterling to hear it while he walks away. "You were amazing, and I'm so proud of you."

"Thanks, darlin'," I tug her closer and plant a firm kiss on her lips.

Is it my imagination, or has Jo been acting like she genuinely wants to be my fiancée? No time to ask her about that, though. It's time for bronc riding, one of my favorite events.

"Yee-hah!" Buck almost screeches. "Are you ready for more, ladies and gents? First up, Clay McKendrick, riding Black Thunder!"

A hush falls over the arena as I settle into the chute, and the crowd waits in anticipation. The silence is electric. The bronc beneath me, Blackout, is all coiled energy and attitude, his muscles twitching as if he can't wait to fly out of the chute either. This is what I live for—the moment right before the gate opens when everything else fades away except the horse and the clock.

"Show 'em what Montana boys are made of!" Jo calls out from the rail, and I catch her eye just long enough to see her cross her fingers. The gesture is so endearingly superstitious that I can't help but grin.

I adjust my grip on Blackout's rein, feeling the familiar weight of the horse between my legs. Black Thunder shifts restlessly, and I can tell he's going to be a handful. Good. I've never been one to back down from a challenge.

"Ready when you are, cowboy," the gate man says.

I nod once. "Let 'er rip."

The gate swings open and the bronc explodes from the chute like he's been shot from a cannon. His first jump nearly sends me sailing over his head, but I recover, and my body finds a rhythm that comes from years of practice and more than a few hard landings. Blackout twists beneath me, his powerful hindquarters launching skyward in a move that has unseated better cowboys than me. I lean back, countering his momentum, my spurs marking the point of each jump as required. This ain't my first rodeo, and Black Thunder seems determined to make me earn every second.

The crowd's roar fades to white noise as I focus entirely on staying centered. Four seconds in, and the bastard changes tactics, spinning hard to the left before launching into a series of stiff-legged jumps that rattle my teeth. My free arm pumps for balance as I spur forward on each jump, keeping time with his rhythm. Six seconds down, two to go.

Black Thunder saves the best for last, executing a perfect sunfish that would make a rodeo photographer weep with joy. His body arcs through the air like a crescent moon, and for a heart-stopping moment I'm damn near vertical, clinging to nothing but leather and determination.

The buzzer sounds just as I feel my grip starting to slip. Eight seconds. I bail off to the left, hitting the dirt with a satisfying thud as the pickup men corral Black Thunder away from the action.

"Eighty-nine point five!" Buck hollers as the scores flash on the board. "That puts Clay McKendrick in first place in both bull riding and saddle bronc!"

The crowd goes wild as Jo blows kisses to me from the stands.

Fake relationship my ass.

Chapter Eleven

Past Shadows

Once the bronc and bull riding events are over, I get excited by something I never expected would interest me—ladies breakaway roping. Jo is participating in that event, so of course, I'll be watching from the stands and cheering for my fiancée. Fake fiancée, Jo would remind me. Whether she still believes that, I can't say.

I settle into my seat, adjusting my hat to shield my eyes from the sun beating down on the stands. The crowd around me buzzes with excitement, but my focus narrows to the chute where Jo is getting ready. She's checking her rope with practiced precision, her movements fluid and confident with that laser-focused look she gets before competing.

"Up next," Buck announces, his voice carrying that special enthusiasm he reserves for events he particularly enjoys, "it's ladies breakaway roping with our first contestant—Jolene Callahan!"

Jo nods to the gate operator, her body coiled like a tight spring as she waits for her moment. When the gate flies open, she springs into action, her horse behaving like the mare is an extension of her own body. The calf bounding ahead while and Jo's rope is already spinning in a perfect circle above her head, the motion so smooth that it seems effortless.

I lean forward in my seat, gripping the metal bench until my knuckles turn white. Watching Jo work mesmerizes me. She's graceful and powerful, every movement executed with absolute precision. She has it all, rolled into one hell of a package. The rope flies true, settling around the calf's neck. Jo's horse plants her feet, and the breakaway string does its job, the rope releasing from her saddle horn as designed. Clean catch, perfect form.

"Time!" the judge calls out.

Buck's voice crackles over the speakers. "Two-point-eight seconds for Jolene Callahan! Ladies and gentlemen, that's yet another arena record for our favorite lady!"

The crowd goes wild again, their cheers reverberating throughout the arena. I'm on my feet before I realize what I'm doing, waving my hat in the air, hollering and whooping like I've just won the lottery. Watching Jo set another arena record feels like hitting the jackpot, for sure. That woman takes my breath away every time I see her in action.

"That's my girl!" I shout, virtually screaming, not giving a damn who hears me. Several cowboys around me chuckle and slap my back in congratulation, like her victory is somehow mine too.

Jo's smile as she exits the arena is pure sunshine, lighting up her whole face in a way that makes me want to kiss her mindless and fuck her out here in the open. I would gladly go to jail for that offense. Jo catches my eye in the stands and tips her hat in my direction, a private acknowledgment that turns me on more than I would've expected. Sizzling heat rushing through my veins.

"Your fiancée's on fire today," a familiar voice proclaims beside me. I turn to see Buck, his microphone temporarily abandoned, sliding into the seat beside mine. "Two arena records in one day. She's making the rest of 'em look like amateurs."

"Jo is extraordinary. Didn't think it was possible to set a time that fast on this arena setup."

Buck's lifts his hat just enough that he can wipe the sweat off his head. "Talent like that don't come along every day. You're a lucky man, Clay."

I am lucky, for sure, but for how long will I have that amazing woman in my life? She thinks this is nothing but a fake engagement for publicity. The question I asked myself a moment ago echoes in my mind now as I watch Jo being congratulated by other competitors. I need to remind myself our romance is strictly for show—a strategic move to boost both our careers and stick it to Brock Sterling. But the way my heart races when she smiles at me feels pretty damn real.

I clear my throat and finally say, "Yeah, I know I'm one lucky bastard."

Buck pats my shoulder before standing. "Gotta get back to the booth. Big announcement coming up in a minute."

He heads back toward the announcers' stand, leaving me alone with my thoughts and the ramifications of his words. *Lucky man.* If only he knew how complicated "lucky" can get.

Jo climbs the bleacher steps while grinning at me, her face aglow from her big victory. Several people stop her along the way to offer congratulations, and she handles every interaction with that perfect blend of gracious acceptance and genuine warmth that makes her so damn appealing.

Once she sits down beside me, I grin and kiss her cheek. "Two arena records in one day. You're turning into a serious show-off."

"Says the man who took first place in two events himself." She bumps my shoulder into hers, and even that casual contact makes my dick rouse. "We make quite the team, don't we, Jo?"

The word "team" hangs in the air between us, loaded with meaning I'm not sure either of us is ready to examine. Before I can respond, Buck's voice reverberates out of the speakers once again.

"Ladies and gentlemen, we have a special announcement from the Professional Rodeo Cowboys Association!"

The crowd quiets, and I feel Jo tense beside me. PRCA announcements during events usually mean something big—new rules, special recognition, or in rare cases, opportunities that can change careers overnight.

A man in a crisp suit and pristine white hat makes his way to the center of the arena, microphone in hand. I recognize him from photos in rodeo magazines—Jim Crawford, one of the PRCA's top executives.

"Thank you, Buck," Crawford says. "I'm here today to announce an exciting new partnership between the PRCA and Western Heritage Brands, one of the fastest-growing lifestyle companies in the country."

Jo's hand finds mine on the bench between us. We intertwine our fingers, holding on tight.

"Western Heritage Brands is launching a nationwide campaign focusing on the authentic spirit of rodeo," Crawford continues, the now-silent arena waiting to hear more. "And they're looking for the perfect couple to be the face of this partnership."

My pulse quickens as Jo squeezes my hand hard enough to make me wince. This must be what Buck was hinting at earlier—the big opportunity that could change everything.

"The selected pair will represent both the PRCA and Western Heritage Brands in a series of national advertisements, promotional appearances, and social media campaigns," Crawford explains, his enthusiasm evident even from this distance. "We're talking print ads, television commercials, billboards—the works. This is the largest promotional deal in PRCA history, folks."

The murmur that ripples through the crowd tells me everyone understands the significance of what Crawford just announced. This isn't just about prize money anymore. It's the kind of exposure that can set up a cowboy and cowgirl for life.

"The campaign will focus on couples who embody the true spirit of rodeo," Crawford continues. "Partnership, dedication, and authentic connection both in and out of the arena. We're looking for riders who can represent not just the sport, but the lifestyle and values that make rodeo America's original sport."

Jo's breathing has become shallow, like mine. This is exactly what we've been working toward without even knowing it—the visibility, the narrative, the story that Buck kept talking about.

"Selection will be based on a combination of factors," Crawford explains. "Competition results, of course, but also marketability, social media presence, and that indefinable quality we call 'rodeo heart.'"

I can feel the energy shift in the crowd as Crawford's words sink in. This is it—the chance to secure more than just my family's ranch, but also a future I never dared dream of. A future with Jo. If she wants that. I'll convince her we belong together, no matter what it takes.

"The deadline for applications is next Friday," Crawford says. "And I'm pleased to announce that the selection committee will be conducting interviews right here at the Houston Livestock Show and Rodeo in two weeks."

Houston. My stomach drops. Jo's ex-husband Tyler lives in Houston and works for a big oil company there. I glance at Jo, but I can't read her expression.

"The winning couple will receive a guaranteed minimum of one-point-five million dollars over the course of the three-year contract!" Crawford exclaims, arms spread wide.

And the crowd erupts in appreciative whistles and applause.

One-point-five million. Holy shit. The number rings in my ears like a church bell on Sunday morning. That kind of money would save the ranch ten times over, with plenty left to modernize the place and expand our breeding program. Hell, I could finally build Dad that accessible cabin by the creek he's always wanted, where he could fish without struggling over rough terrain.

I steal another glance at Jo, whose face has gone carefully blank—her competition face. I bet she's already plotting a strategy to catapult us into the winner's circle.

"Applications are available at the PRCA tent," Crawford finishes with a wide smile. "Good luck to all our competitors!"

The moment Crawford exits the arena, everyone around us suddenly starts chattering away, talking at once. I can practically feel the calculation happening in every cowboy and cowgirl's mind—who's dating whom, who might make a good partner, who has the best chance at that this fortune-changing opportunity.

"Clay," Jo says slowly, her voice barely audible over the crowd. "We need to talk."

Aw, shit. Those are the words no man wants to hear from his girl. Yep, my happy balloon just burst.

Chapter Twelve

Broken Trust

y life had been going pretty damn good lately, especially at the Parker County events. I rode both a bronc and a bull to my best times ever. Jo had similar experiences, and I couldn't be prouder of her for nailing all her events. Brock and Maddie might've tried to ruin us both, but their efforts went down in flames. Today, I'm on my way to another arena—in Pretty Prairie, Kansas—but it won't involve me or any other men. The ladies will have their turn in a women's only rodeo.

Naturally, I'll be there to cheer on my "fake" fiancée. Our relationship doesn't feel phony to me.

I'm halfway to my destination when my phone bleeps, indicating a new message. I pull over onto the shoulder to open up the text—and everything inside me freezes. The photo on my phone screen might as well be a death sentence.

"Clay McKendrick and Jo Callahan's Fake Romance EXPOSED!"

The screaming headline is splashed across the social media feed of *Rodeo Dish Magazine,* an outlet I've never heard of. Below that is a grainy image that seems to show me handing Jo money outside that honky-tonk in Durango a few months ago. The caption reads: "Sources confirm McKendrick paid Callahan for publicity stunt engagement. Audio recording reveals their scheme."

My blood turns to ice water as I scroll through the comments that are flooding in faster than I can read them. The rodeo community is tearing us apart like vultures pouncing on roadkill.

"Always knew something was fishy about those two."

"Poor Clay, getting used by that conniving bitch."

"Fake engagement for fake champions."

"What's next, fake babies?"

Every comment slams into me like a physical blow, but it's the damage already done to our reputations that has me gripping the steering wheel until my knuckles turn white. The PRCA campaign selection is in three days. This attempt to smear us both couldn't have come at a worse time.

My phone rings, making me jerk. Jo's name flashes on the screen. I answer before the first ring finishes. "I saw it. Feel like hunting down the prick who wrote that slanderous article so I can wallop him until he's bloody."

"Clay, please don't do anything rash, at least until we figure out what's really going on. But I've heard the WPRA might investigate and possibly…" Jo's voice broke near the end, and that single syllable carried more pain than I've ever heard from her. "They might bar me from competing in the Pretty Prairie event or any future events."

"What?" I snarl, glaring at the article that I still have displayed on my phone. "Nobody will stop you from competing. I'll make sure of that. Whatever it takes."

"There are two different versions of the Rodeo Dish article that are circulating." Her breathing is uneven, like she's been running. Or crying. "Someone's determined to turn us against each other. Clay, I swear to God, I didn't do this. I would never—"

"I know, I know." The words come out rougher than I intended, though gentler than my snarling a minute ago. Whatever complications we've had between us, Jo is not the type to stab someone in the back. "This has Brock and Maddie's fingerprints all over it."

"There's allegedly a recording." Jo sniffles, her voice tight with panic. "They claim to have audio of us discussing the fake engagement. How is that even possible?"

My mind races back to that day at the stables when Jo first announced our engagement to Sterling.

Had someone been listening? Recording? These days, with AI and other shit like that, anything is possible. The thought makes my skin crawl.

"Could've been anybody with a phone, Jo." I set my phone on the dashboard so I can have both hands on the wheel as I back out of the gravel lot and onto the road. The women's rodeo suddenly feels a million miles away. "Question is, how do we prove the image is an AI fake?"

"We can't," all but moans. "By the time we find tech experts to analyze it, the damage will be done. The PRCA selection committee will have moved on to other couples."

I slam my palm against the steering wheel, the sharp pain grounding me for a moment. "There's got to be something we can do. This is our shot, Jo. The prize money could change everything for both of us."

"You think I don't know that?" She blows her nose. "I've been working toward something like this my entire career. And now it's all falling apart because of some doctored photos and bogus audio."

The line goes quiet except for the sound of her ragged breathing. I can picture her pacing, probably wearing a hole in whatever floor she's standing on. It's what she does when she's cornered.

I pull over onto the shoulder. "Where are you, Jo?"

"At the arena in Pretty Prairie." I can hear the echo of her boots on concrete in the background. "I came early to warm up, then saw this mess explode on my phone. Everyone's staring at me, Clay. Like I'm some kind of fraud."

"Stay there. I'm fifteen minutes out." I check my mirrors and pull back onto the highway, pressing the gas pedal harder than necessary. "Don't talk to anyone about this until we're together."

"Too late. Maddie's already here, strutting around like she's won the lottery." Jo's voice drops to a whisper. "She just walked by and asked how much I charged you for my 'services.' I nearly decked her."

My jaw clenches so hard I can hear my teeth grinding. "Don't give her the satisfaction. That's exactly what they want—for one of us to lose our cool and make this situation even worse. We need to stay calm and figure this out together."

"But Clay, what if there's nothing to figure out? What if this is just…over?"

Something in her tone makes me swallow hard. She's not just talking about the campaign anymore.

"Nothing's over," I assure her with more conviction than I feel. "I'll be there in ten. *Wait for me.*"

I end the call and jam the accelerator down to the floorboards. My truck eats up the miles between us, but it still isn't fast enough. My mind races through options, each one more desperate than the last. We could deny everything, but without proof, it's our word against doctored evidence. We could try to prove the photos and audio are fake, but that takes time we don't have. Or we could…

The thought hits me like a lightning bolt. It's crazy enough that it might actually work. What if we stop running from this mess and lean into it instead? What if we tell the truth? That yes, our engagement started as a publicity stunt, but somewhere along the way it became real. For me, it's always been real because I'm in love with Jolene Callahan.

Right now, I need to get to Jo.

I pull into the arena parking lot with gravel spraying behind my tires. The place is buzzing with activity despite the early hour—trailers being unloaded, horses being exercised, competitors preparing for what should be Jo's moment to shine. Instead, she's dealing with a nightmare.

I find her exactly where I expected—behind the stock pens, pacing like a caged wildcat. Her hat's pulled low, but I can see the tension in every line of her body, the way her shoulders curl forward like she's bracing for a physical blow. When she spots me, her posture changes. She straightens up as if drawing strength from my presence.

"Clay," she says, blowing out a gusty breath.

I close the distance between us in a few long strides, pulling her into my arms without hesitation. She stiffens for half a second before melting against me, her face mashed into my shirt. I can feel her trembling, and that realization ignites a fierce protective instinct within me.

"We'll fix this, darlin'," I whisper into her hair, breathing in the familiar scent of her shampoo. "I promise you nobody will wreck your rodeo dreams."

She pulls back just enough to gaze up at me, her green eyes rimmed with red. "How? The selection committee meets tomorrow. By the time we get lawyers involved or tech experts to prove the photos are doctored, they'll have already chosen someone else."

"Then we don't try to prove they're fake." A plan is crystallizing in my mind even as I speak. "We get ahead of this thing instead of chasing behind it."

Jo frowns, wiping at her eyes with the back of her hand. "What do you mean?"

"We tell our story first. The real story." I cup her face in my hands, forcing her to meet my gaze. "We admit that yeah, our engagement started as a business arrangement. But we tell them what happened after—how it became something neither of us expected."

For the first time since I've known her, Jolene Callahan seems uncertain and vulnerable. I take a deep breath, knowing whatever I say next will change everything between us. "Jo, I'm in love with you. And I'm pretty sure you feel the same way, though I get why you don't want to admit it. But I would never ditch you the way your ex-husband did. When it comes to love, I'm a lifetime kind of guy."

A single tear slides down her cheek, and I catch it with my thumb. "I won't lie to you, Clay. You mean a lot to me, but I'm not ready for a serious relationship, not yet."

"I know that, baby. And it's okay. I can wait as long as you need—even forever." I wiggle my eyebrows and grin. "It might be fun keep pretending to pretend we have a fake relationship. Just imagine what a field day Rodeo Dish Magazine will have with that."

A laugh bursts out of her, sloppy but real, and it's the most beautiful sound I've heard all day. And suddenly, I know we'll find a way out of this mess. But I'll need to convince Jo that the plan I just came up with can save our skins.

Chapter Thirteen

Rock Bottom

My pickup coughs and sputters like it's on its last breath as I pull into the McKendrick ranch driveway. The scandal has followed me all the way from Texas to Montana, my phone blowing up with notifications I can't bear to read anymore. I kill the engine and sit for a moment, staring at the weathered farmhouse where four generations of McKendricks have lived, loved, and struggled. The place looks tired in the fading light, like it knows what's coming.

Yesterday, I heard the WPRA allowed Jo to compete in the Pretty Prairie event. They realized the rumors about me and Jo are just that—rumors. Despite all the drama, she scored several more wins. I'm so damn proud of her.

I sigh wistfully. "Home sweet home."

Thunder's nickering in the trailer reminds me I've got responsibilities that don't give a hoot about my broken heart. After Pretty Prairie, Jo took off for another WPRA event without even saying goodbye and competed in several more women's events over the past three weeks. But I'm not as worried about that or my tattered reputation as I probably should be. Sure, I think about Jo more than I should. But she's the one who bailed on me.

I climb out of the pickup and begin the familiar routine of unloading my horse, the physical labor a welcome distraction from the storm in my head.

Dad's sitting on the porch when I lead Thunder toward the barn. He doesn't call out to me. No, he just rocks the porch swing while calmly watching me disappear into the barn. Why did Dad seem...pleased? Or maybe it's resignation because his son fucked up royally. But as I head for Thunder's box stall, a figure emerges from the shadows across from me.

It's Jolene Callahan.

Her auburn hair catches the last rays of sunlight streaming through the barn's open doors. She's clutching her hat in her hands like a shield. The sight of Jo, here on my family's land, hits me like a bolt of lightning. Maybe I'm delirious. But no, this feels real.

"Jo, ah, what are you doing here?"

She takes a tentative step forward, her boots scuffing against the hay-strewn floor. "I had to see you. After everything that's happened, I couldn't just leave things the way they were."

"You ran out on me, abandoned our plan, left me in the lurch."

Jo hunches her shoulders, biting her upper lip. "Please, can we talk?"

Thunder snorts and tosses his head, sensing the tension between us. I lead him into his stall, buying myself time to process seeing her here. She followed me home. All the way to Montana.

"How'd you even find this place?" I ask, latching the stall door.

"Buck gave me directions." A ghost of a smile tightens her face briefly, but it doesn't reach her eyes. "Said you'd need someone to talk sense into you after...after everything."

I lean against the stall door. "Buck should mind his own business."

"He cares about you." Jo steps closer, and I can smell her sweet floral perfume. "We both do, Clay. And I...miss you."

That last part hangs in the air between us, loaded with everything we haven't said to each other. The barn feels too small suddenly, the walls closing in as I try to figure out what to say next.

"The PRCA called me yesterday," she says. "They wanted my side of the story."

"Your side? Two of us were involved, you know. What did you tell the PRCA?"

"The truth." Her eyes meet mine, her expression placid. "Told them our engagement started as a strategy but became something real along the way. That whatever mistakes we made, the feelings between us aren't fake."

I study her, unsure of how I should feel right now. "You told them that?"

"I told them everything, Clay. About the honky-tonk, about Sterling's threats, about how we needed each other for different reasons but ended up needing each other for the same one." She sets her hat on a hay bale and steps closer. "I told them I'm in love with you."

The words hit me so hard that I stumble backward half a step. "Jo... are you sure about this? I mean, you ran away the last time we saw each other."

"I'm so sorry about that, Clay. I know it's complicated. I know the timing is terrible with everything seeming to fall apart." She lifts her chin, her stance defiant. "But I couldn't let you think that any of this was just business for me. Not anymore. I love you, Clay. I'll say it ten more times if that's what it takes for you to believe me."

Thunder whickers softly from his stall. It's the only sound in the barn as I struggle to find the right words. This woman who's turned my world upside down is standing in front of me, laying her heart bare, and I'm frozen like a greenhorn on his first bronc.

"The bank called yesterday," I finally say, my voice rough. "They're moving forward with foreclosure proceedings."

Jo flinches. "Clay, I don't know what to say except I'm sorry. That doesn't mean much, though."

"Four generations of McKendricks managed to keep this place afloat through droughts, floods, and market crashes. Then I come along and lose it all." A bitter laugh spills out of me. "Some legacy I'm leaving."

"You can't give up yet," Jo declares, taking another step toward me. "We can still fight. Together."

"Fight with what? Our reputations are in tatters. The PRCA campaign is gone. I've got maybe two months before the bank forecloses." I shove a hand through my hair, frustration burning inside me. "I've got nothing left to fight with, Jo."

She strides up to me, the distance between us abruptly erased. The determination flashing in those green eyes gives me an ache in my chest. "You've got me, Clay McKendrick. Whether you want me or not. And I will never walk away from you again. Please believe me."

And I do believe her. So, I drag her into my arms and kiss her like the world's about to end, holding nothing back as I devour her mouth and grasp her ass roughly. A jolt of lust hits me, and I drag her down onto a pile of straw. We tear each other's clothes off, not giving a damn about ripping anything. I've just freed one breast when I hear something that stops me.

The distinctive sound of someone clearing their throat.

Jo and I freeze.

"Not that I wanna interrupt, but your ma has dinner ready."

"Dad?" I toss my shirt to cover up Jo's tits, then spring to my knees and gape at my father over my shoulder. "Give us a minute, okay?"

He grins. "Sure thing, kiddo. Guess we better put you and Jo in the big bedroom tonight."

My father walks out of the barn, limping but much stronger on his feet than he used to be. The PRCA pledged a good chunk of change to the fundraising campaign I set up for my dad. He groused about letting family and friends do that, but we all know he's secretly grateful.

"Oh, by the way," Jo says. "The PRCA didn't cancel our interview. They still want to see us tomorrow in Billings."

I gape at her in disbelief. "That's unbelievable news."

"Turns out, people love a redemption story even more than they love a scandal." A hint of her familiar smirk reappears. "Buck's been working his connections, telling everyone how Sterling and Maddie set us up. Apparently, the PRCA brass are more interested in authentic love stories than perfect PR campaigns."

My mouth falls open. "They believe us?"

"Oh, more than that—they think we're exactly what they're looking for. A real couple who found love in the middle of the chaos." Jo slings her arms around my neck, her toes barely touching the ground since I'm considerably taller. "They want to hear our story, Clay. The whole truth and more."

I shake my head, not daring to hope. "Even if that's true, it doesn't solve the ranch problem. Two months isn't enough time for the fundraising money to grow into a big enough pile even if we somehow land the contract. Besides, my stubborn dad won't let us include the ranch in the fundraising campaign."

"Oh, you just let me handle that." Jo's smile turns mysterious. "I have a way with stubborn McKendrick men, as you well know."

Suddenly, Dad's voice carries across the barnyard. "Clay! You got company! And we're all getting' tired of waiting for dinner because of you lovebirds."

I glance toward the barn doors to see Buck Hawkins striding toward us, looking more put-together than I've ever seen him. Gone is the weathered Stetson and faded jeans, replaced by a crisp white shirt and a bolo tie that catches the fading sunlight.

"There you two are." Bucks voice echoes through the barn. "Been looking all over for you."

Jo squeezes my arm before stepping back, putting a respectable distance between us as our newest guest approaches. "Perfect timing as always, Buck."

He grins, tipping his hat at Jo before turning his attention to me. "Clay, son, we need to talk business. The kind that might just save this ranch of yours."

I glance between them. "What's going on here? You two cooking something up behind my back?"

"Not behind your back," Jo says quickly. "We wanted to present you with options. Real ones."

Buck leans against a support beam, his expression more serious than I've ever seen it. "Clay, what do you know about syndicated broadcasting rights for rodeo events?"

"Not much. Why do you ask?"

"Because I've been in this business for thirty years, and I've got connections you wouldn't believe." He pulls out a folded document from his shirt pocket. "Ever since this mess with Sterling started, I've been making calls. Turns out, there's a group of investors looking to create a new rodeo broadcast network—something grittier, more authentic than the polished stuff on the big networks."

Jo steps forward. "They want real stories, Clay. Cowboys and cowgirls who've struggled, who've earned their place through blood and sweat, not family connections and sponsor money."

"And they want you and Jo to be the face of it," Buck finishes, his wrinkles creasing into a grin. "Not only as competitors, but as hosts. A husband-and-wife team telling the real stories behind the rides."

My head spins while I try to grasp what they're saying. "Husband and wife?"

Jo throws an arm around my waist. "We'd have to actually get married for the contract, Clay. Real marriage, not for show this time. Shouldn't be a problem since we're in love."

"Uh, yeah, that's true."

The barn goes dead quiet except for Thunder's occasional snort and the settling of old wood. I can't stop staring at both of them like they've lost their ever-loving minds.

I feel my brow furrow. "You're asking me to marry you for a business deal?"

"No," Jo says firmly, stepping closer again. "I'm asking you to marry me because I love you. The business deal is just a bonus that happens to solve both our problems at the same time."

Her words hit me like a sledgehammer to the chest. I've been so focused on trying to separate the real from the fake between us that I never stopped to consider she might be dealing with the same confusion.

"Jo, I—"

She holds up a hand, cutting me off. "Let me finish, okay?"

"Yeah, sure."

She takes a shaky breath, and I can see her hands trembling slightly. "I know this is crazy. I know the timing is terrible."

Buck clears his throat awkwardly. "Maybe I should give you two some privacy—"

"Stay," I say without taking my eyes off Jo. "If we're doing this, we're doing it with all our cards on the table."

"With you, I'm ready for anything."

Chapter Fourteen
The Comeback Trail

Jo and I don't intend to waste much time on beginning our road to a shared comeback. It's ready, set, go—right now. My family has signed on to help in whatever way they can too. So here we are, gathered in my family's kitchen while Dad makes his famous blueberry pancakes and my sister Sarah fusses over Jo like she's already part of the family.

"The network wants us to start filming next month," Jo explains, spreading a topographical map across the kitchen table. "They're thinking we'll showcase smaller rodeos first, the ones that don't get national attention but have incredible talent."

"And they're really offering enough to stop the foreclosure?" Dad asks, flipping a pancake with practiced ease despite his leg brace. The skepticism in his voice is fair. We've had too many false hopes these past few years.

"Not just stop it," Buck explains, helping himself to coffee. "The advance alone is enough to clear the debt and have some operating capital left over. Once the show starts airing, you'll have steady income coming in."

Sarah leans over the map, her finger tracing a route through Montana and down into Wyoming. "They want to start in our backyard, huh?"

I shrug, sipping my coffee. "Makes sense. Some of the best unknown talent competes right here. Plus, it gives us home-field advantage for the first episodes."

Jo nods, tucking a strand of hair behind her ear. "The producers think starting with familiar territory will help us find our rhythm before we hit the bigger circuits."

"And when exactly is this wedding supposed to happen?" Dad asks, sliding a stack of pancakes in front of me. His expression is neutral, but I note the hint of a smile tugging at the corners of his mouth.

Jo and I exchange glances. We haven't actually discussed the timeline yet. Everything's happened so fast since we left Billings with signed contracts in hand. The network executives practically fell over themselves when we walked in together. Our romance has proved to be exactly what they were looking for.

My mom walks into the kitchen, holding our landline phone to her ear. "All the neighbors are dying to know about the wedding too. Phone's been ringing off the hook."

"It'll be soon," Jo confirms. "The network wants us married before filming starts. Something about authenticity in our on-screen chemistry. But Clay and I still haven't discussed the details of our wedding."

"How soon *is* soon?" Sarah asks, raising her eyebrows while she pours syrup over her pancakes.

I reach for Jo's hand across the table, intertwining our fingers. "How does two weeks sound, darlin'?"

Dad's fork pauses halfway to his mouth. "Two weeks? Son, that's barely enough time to plan a proper wedding." He winks. "That's what your mom always claimed, anyway."

Jo clears her throat deliberately. "We don't need anything fancy. Just family and a handful of close friends. Maybe we could do it right here on the ranch."

Getting married on McKendrick land, where four generations of my family have lived and loved…It feels like kismet.

"The old oak down by the creek would be perfect," Sarah suggests, her eyes alight excitement. She's always loved party planning. "We could string lights through the branches, set up tables on the flat ground by the water."

Buck grins, slapping his knee. "Now that sounds like a proper cowboy wedding. None of that fancy hotel ballroom nonsense."

"I love it," Jo breathes, squeezing my hand. "Sounds perfect, doesn't it, Clay?"

Dad sets down his fork, abruptly serious. "You sure about this, son? Marriage is a big step, even when it starts with the best intentions. And you two have been through hell these past few weeks. No offense, Jo, but you did run out on Clay for a while there."

I can feel everyone's eyes on me—and Jo. Dad's not wrong. We're moving fast, maybe too fast. But when I look at Jo, sitting in my family's kitchen like she belongs there, I've never been more certain of anything in my life.

"Yeah, Dad, I'm sure. Sometimes you just know." I clasp Jo's hand, and she smiles sweetly. "Jo had her reasons for leaving, but I always knew she'd come back to me. I know all about her reasons for what she did, and I just need you all to trust me on this. Jo means to stay with me for good."

"That's right," Jo concurs. Her eyes meet mine, and the love I see there makes everything else fade away. The scandals, the setbacks, even the foreclosure notice. Those are only distant problems compared to the certainty I feel right now. "Besides, we've already been through the 'for worse' part. Might as well stick around for the 'for better.' Right?"

That breaks the tension, and Dad chuckles as he pushes away from the table. "I had to test you two, that's all. But I could tell from the start it's true love, just like Meryl and me."

"Yeah, I figured you were testing us. That's what Grams and Pop did when you and mom wanted to get married."

Dad slaps me on the shoulder. "Well then, sounds like we've got a wedding to plan. I'll need to dust off my good boots."

Jo gnaws on her bottom lip. "And I'll need to find a dress. Two weeks doesn't give me much time for shopping."

"That's where I come in." Sarah snatches up her phone. "I know the perfect place in Billings. We can drive up tomorrow."

"Sarah, I couldn't ask you to—"

"You aren't asking, I'm telling." Sarah gives Jo a quick, firm hug. "Besides, you're about to be my sister. Consider it my wedding gift."

The word "sister" brings a flush to Jo's cheeks. I love seeing her this way, no longer the tough barrel racer but now just a woman getting hitched. She's been alone for so long, fighting her own battles, that having family rally around her seems to catch her off guard in the best possible way.

Buck drains his coffee mug and sets it down with a decisive thunk. "While you ladies are handling the dress situation, Clay and I need to start making calls. We've got a list of rodeos to line up for the first season, and we need to start securing filming permits yesterday." He pulls out a small notebook from his pocket, flipping it open to reveal pages of scribbled notes. "The network wants at least ten locations confirmed before they send the camera crew."

"I could help with that," Dad offers, gathering empty plates. "Got some old friends on the circuit who might be willing to let you film at their events."

"Wow, Buck." I shake my head in disbelief. "Thank you so much. Every connection helps."

Jo reaches across the table and gently takes Buck's notebook, scanning his list. "Cody Stampede should definitely be on here. And the Livingston Roundup. Both have incredible local talent that deserves the spotlight."

"Good thinking," Buck agrees, jotting down additional notes. "The network wants authentic stories—cowboys and cowgirls who've been overlooked by the big sponsors but have the heart and skill to make it at the highest levels."

"That's us," I say with a laugh. "Overlooked but with a ton of heart and skill."

Jo grins at me. "Speak for yourself, McKendrick. I've got two arena records now."

"And I've got a fake engagement scandal under my belt," I counter. "Between the two of us, we're reality TV gold."

Sarah glances up from her phone, where she's been frantically texting. "Speaking of reality TV, what are you going to do about Sterling and Maddie? They're still out there spreading poison."

The mention of those two makes my jaw clench automatically. "Let them talk. Truth has a way of coming out eventually."

Buck raises one finger, his expression turning mischievous. "Actually, I might have some news on that front. Word is, the PRCA recently completed their own investigation into the doctored photos and fake audio. After detailed analysis, they agreed it was all bogus. Seems they don't appreciate being made fools of, and they've got better tech experts than we could ever afford."

Jo leans forward, her eyes alight with curiosity. "What sort of investigation?"

"Forensic analysis of digital evidence, interviews with anyone who might've had access to recording equipment at the venues where we competed, stuff like that." Buck's grin widens. "Turns out, Sterling's been a little too comfortable throwing his weight around with PRCA officials. They're not inclined to protect him if he's been playing dirty."

Dad refills his coffee mug, sitting down beside me. "So, Buck, you're saying this whole mess might actually work in Clay and Jo's favor?"

"Could be. Nothing the rodeo community loves more than seeing a bully get his comeuppance. If Sterling and his girlfriend get caught red-handed, it might change everything for Clay and Jo."

Her eyes meet mine across the table, a silent understanding passing between us. We've been through the fire together, and somehow, we're still standing.

"Even if they do get caught," Jo says, "we can't build our future on Sterling's downfall. We need to focus on making this show something special—something that matters to the rodeo community."

Buck taps his pencil against the notebook. "This isn't just about you two anymore. It's about all those cowboys and cowgirls out there struggling to make ends meet while chasing their dreams. Your story could give them hope."

"You know what?" I say, pushing back from the table and standing up. "Let's do this right. Not just the wedding, but everything. The show, the message we're sending, all of it."

Jo rises with me. "What do you have in mind?"

"We make this the most honest thing rodeo's ever seen. No sugar-coating, no manufactured drama. Just real cowboys and cowgirls telling their stories." I gesture toward the window, where the ranch spreads out under the Montana sky. "We show what it really means to fight for something you love."

Sarah claps her hands. "I love it. Like a documentary series but with genuine heart."

"And actual ratings potential," Buck adds pragmatically. "The network's going to eat this up. Authentic always sells."

I can't believe the way everyone I love is working so hard to make this happen for me and Jo. As for Brock and Maddie…We aren't interested in payback.

We want justice.

Chapter Fifteen
Truth and Consequences

Jo and I have everything to lose if our plan goes sideways. The press conference room at the Las Vegas Convention Center is packed tighter than a rodeo chute on championship night. Every reporter, photographer, and rodeo insider who could wrangle their way in is here, hungry for the next chapter in what Buck's been calling "the scandal of the decade." I can feel Jo's hand trembling slightly in mine as we wait behind the curtain.

"You ready for this?" I whisper, giving her fingers a gentle squeeze.

She looks up at me. "Ready as I'll ever be. You've got the evidence?"

I pat my jacket pocket where the flash drive feels like it weighs a hundred pounds. "Right here. Everything Maddie's cousin sent over."

Turns out, Maddie Vale's own flesh and blood couldn't stomach the scheme she and Sterling cooked up. Her cousin works in tech support at Sterling's sponsor company and had access to their email accounts. One anonymous message to Buck later, and we had everything we needed—the original photos before they were doctored, email exchanges planning the whole setup, even receipts for the voice actor they hired to create that fake audio.

"Remember," Jo says, her voice remarkably calm, "we stick to the facts. No accusations we can't back up."

I adjust my bolo tie, which Jo had picked out for me. I'm wearing a proper suit for once, and it feels as strange as the first time I climbed on a bronc. But Jo insisted we should look the part today—professional, polished, unshakeable.

Buck pokes his head through the curtain. "They're ready for you. And Clay? Sterling just arrived with his lawyer."

Perfect. Let him try to squirm out of this one.

As we step out into the blazing lights, the room falls silent except for the rapid-fire clicking of camera shutters. I scan the crowd and spot Brock Sterling immediately—he's sitting in the front row with some slick-looking lawyer in an expensive suit, both of them wearing expressions that could instigate a deep freeze in hell.

Maddie's nowhere to be seen, which tells me everything I need to know about loyalty among thieves.

Jo and I take our seats at the podium table, and I'm struck by how composed she is. The woman who once kicked me out of her truck and handed me cab fare has transformed into someone who could command any room she enters. Seeing her this way makes me want to drag her behind the curtains so I can do dirty things to her.

"Thank you all for coming," Jo begins, her voice carrying clearly through the packed room. "Clay and I called this press conference to set the record straight about recent allegations regarding our relationship."

A reporter near the back raises her hand. "Miss Callahan, are you denying that your engagement was fabricated for publicity?"

I lean forward, folding my hands on the table. "We're not denying anything. That's why we're here—to tell the truth, all of it. We'll take questions in a moment." I gesture for the reporter to wait. "First, we have information to share."

Jo squeezes my thigh under the table as she faces the crowd. "For the past several weeks, there have been accusations that Clay and I fabricated our relationship for publicity and financial gain. Today, we're here to present evidence that not only proves these accusations are false but also reveals who orchestrated this smear campaign against us."

The room buzzes with whispers as I connect the flash drive to the laptop. The projector screen behind us flickers to life, displaying the first email from Brock to Maddie.

"What you're seeing," I explain, "is correspondence between Brock Sterling and Maddie Vale, detailing their plan to discredit us before the PRCA campaign selection."

Sterling's face has gone pale. His lawyer is already on his feet, whispering frantically in his ear as the evidence is displayed for everyone to see.

"Need I remind everyone," Jo continues, "that manipulating images and creating false audio to damage competitors' reputations violates multiple PRCA regulations and potentially constitutes defamation."

I click to the next slide—a side-by-side comparison of the original photo and the doctored version showing me supposedly handing Jo money. The timestamps and metadata are highlighted, proving the manipulation.

"As you can see," I explain, pointing to the screen, "this image was altered to suggest a financial transaction between us, when the original clearly shows me handing Jo her hat after she dropped it outside the honky-tonk in Durango."

The room erupts with questions, cameras flashing like lightning in a summer storm. Sterling's lawyer is now on his feet, waving his hands. "This is outrageous! My client categorically denies any involvement in—"

"Save it for court," Buck hollers from the other side of the room. He strides toward the podium with the confidence of a man who's seen it all and then some. "Ladies and gentlemen, as a PRCA representative for over thirty years, I've witnessed my share of rivalries, but this crosses every line we have in professional rodeo."

The lawyer sputters, but Buck isn't finished. He produces a folder and slaps it down on the podium beside us.

"The PRCA Ethics Committee has reviewed the evidence independently and reached their own conclusions," Buck announces, his expression solemn. "Effective immediately, Brock Sterling and Maddie Vale are suspended from competition pending a full disciplinary hearing."

The room explodes. Reporters leap to their feet, shouting questions over each other while cameras flash like strobe lights. In the chaos, I see Sterling's face contort with rage, his lawyer desperately trying to control him. But it's too late. Brock shoves past his attorney and storms toward our table, pointing an accusing finger.

"This is a setup!" he shouts, his eyes bulging, his hands fisted as he shakes them violently. "You think you can just waltz in here with some doctored emails and take me down? Do you know who I am? This is a disgrace!"

Security moves in quickly, but not before Jo rises to her feet, perfectly calm despite the chaos raging around us. "We know exactly who you are, Brock. That's the problem."

The guards flank Sterling, who's now red-faced and snarling about lawsuits. Reporters shout questions over each other, and cameras flash like strobe lights. Amid the chaos, I spot Brock's face, contort with rage, and his lawyer desperately trying to control him. But it's too late. Brock shoves past his attorney, nearly knocking the guy down, and storms toward our table.

He jabs an accusing finger at me. "You'll get yours, McKendrick. Mark my words."

Security moves in swiftly, taking control of the situation. The guards escort Sterling out, his protests fading as the doors swing shut behind him. A moment of stunned silence follows before the room erupts again. Reporters shout questions from every direction. I catch Buck's eye across the podium, and his slight nod tells me we've won this round.

"One at a time, please," Jo says, raising her hands to calm the frenzy. Her voice carries the same natural authority that first drew me to her.

A reporter from Western Rodeo Magazine stands up. "Now that Sterling and Vale have been suspended, what does this mean for you two and the PRCA campaign?"

Jo glances at me, and I take the cue. "Nothing's changed. We have amazing opportunities ahead of us, and we look forward to our future together."

Another reporter jumps in. "What about the wedding, Ms. Callahan? Is that still happening?"

"The wedding is very much on."

Buck steps forward again, clearing his throat. "I've got a statement from the PRCA selection committee." He unfolds an official-looking paper. "In light of recent events and the evidence presented today, the PRCA is pleased to announce that Clay McKendrick and Jolene Callahan have been selected as the featured couple for the Western Heritage Brands national campaign."

The room goes dead silent for a heartbeat before erupting into chaos again. I feel Jo's hand squeeze mine tightly. We did it. We actually did it.

"The selection committee was impressed not only by their competitive achievements," Buck continues, raising his voice over the commotion, "but by their integrity in bringing this matter to light. They represent the authentic spirit of rodeo that Western Heritage Brands wants to showcase."

A reporter from Rodeo Today shouts over the noise. "What's the timeline for the campaign launch?"

Buck grins. "Filming begins next month, with the first commercials airing during the National Finals Rodeo broadcast. But in the meantime, these two consummate champions will be competing in every rodeo they can find."

He's not exaggerating. Jo and I both agreed to a crazy schedule. Getting back to basics, to what we do the best, feels like coming home after a long time away.

Can't wait to hear those wedding bells.

Chapter Sixteen

The Final Showdown

The Las Vegas rodeo turns out to be an incredible experience, and nobody mentions Brock or Maddie. They've become pariahs in the rodeo world. But Jo and I are on fire everywhere we go, setting our own records as well as PRCA records too. All the drama and stress of the past few months has been burned away, leaving only pure skill and determination. Jo sets another barrel racing record—her third this season—while I manage to stay on a bull that's sent five other cowboys to the dirt in under four seconds.

"Ladies and gentlemen," Buck's voice echoes across the arena as I dust myself off, "that's an eighty-nine point ride for Clay McKendrick! That puts him in first place going into the final round!"

The crowd goes crazy. Jo leaps to her feet, hat in the air, whooping like a wild woman. The sight of her celebrating my success makes me start whooping too.

After the competition ends, we meet up behind the stock pens, away from the crowds and cameras. Adrenaline still courses through my veins, but I feel something else too—a sense of completion that has nothing to do with scores.

"We make a hell of a team, don't we?" Jo says, leaning against the fence rail. Her hair's come loose from her ponytail, and I see a smudge of dirt on her cheek from where she hugged me. "You ride the broncs and bulls to record times while I rock the barrel racing and team roping."

"We're the best for sure," I agree, reaching out to brush the dirt away with my thumb. "Think we can keep this up for the next fifty years or so?"

Her eyes widen slightly at the implication, and her lids flutter. "Fifty years? That's a long time, McKendrick."

"Not long enough." Looking at her now—flushed with victory, eyes sparkling with happiness—I can't imagine a future that doesn't have her in it. Jo Callahan has become my other half, my soul mate, and I don't care how corny that sounds.

"Clay?" Jo's voice pulls me back to the present. She's watching me with those keen green eyes that don't miss a thing. "Where'd you go just now?"

I take her hand, running my thumb over her engagement ring—the real one I bought her last month, not the costume jewelry we used for show. "Just thinking about how different things would be if Sterling hadn't tried to sabotage us."

She nudges me with her shoulder, smiling softly. "You mean if we'd never faked an engagement?"

"Exactly."

Once we're done for the day, We head back to our hotel, where a sexy suite awaits us. The view out the floor to ceiling windows is stunning, and a huge bed offers silk sheets and a bottle of champagne chilling in a bucket. Neither of us needs to express our desires out loud. We strip naked and jump into bed, raring to go, so hot for each other that I swear steam is coming out of my ears.

Jo's skin feels like silk beneath my hands as I pull her against me, months of tension and uncertainty dissolving into pure need. Her mouth finds mine, hungry and demanding, and I lose myself in the taste of her—sweet victory mixed with something uniquely Jo that I've been craving since that first night in her truck.

"God, Clay," she breathes against my lips, her fingers tangling in my hair. "I've been wanting this all day, watching you ride that bull like you owned the world."

"That turned you on big time, hey?" I trail kisses down her throat while I explore every curve of her body that I've memorized in my dreams. She arches beneath me, every soft sound she makes driving me closer to the edge.

She lightly scrapes her nails over my shoulders. "Nothing sexier than a cowboy who knows how to handle eight seconds of fury." Her voice catches as I slide between her thighs, finding her already slick and ready for me. "Oh God, yes, ride me like a wild bull, Clay. Fuck me hard and never stop."

"Damn, baby, I need to come inside you so bad." But force myself to take my time exploring every inch of her luscious body, savoring every gasp and shudder as I circle her clit with my finger and rub my palm into her cleft. She's already so wet that her juices coat my skin, and the scent of her drives me crazy. The way she responds to my touch, so open and uninhibited, makes my own need almost painful.

"Clay, please," she begs, her hips rising to meet my hand. "I need you inside me."

"Patience, darlin'," I whisper against her breast before pulling a nipple into my mouth. The taste of her skin, salty and sweet in a way that's purely Jo, drives me wild. "We've got all night."

"Don't want patience. Want you fucking me *now*."

I rise onto my knees, my stiff cock waving like a flagpole, and roughly flip her over. Then I give her sweet ass a slap. She gasps. I position myself above her, holding my dick in position, and finally thrust inside her deeply. "Christ, Jo, you feel incredible. So fucking wet, so velvety smooth, my cock fits inside you like a glove."

I set a fast rhythm, clutching her hips, pounding into her hard while she cries out over and over, begging me to never stop. I grunt and growl and slam into her even harder and faster while the wet slapping every time our bodies collide fills the air. The champagne sits forgotten as we lose ourselves in each other, months of pretending and uncertainty finally giving way to something real and raw and completely honest.

"I love you," she gasps, wrapping her legs around my hips, her need becoming more urgent. "Not for the cameras, not for the contracts. Just...you."

Those words push me over the edge in a way I never expected. Her inner muscles clench around me in pulsating waves, and I slide one hand between us to circle her clit as I growl, "I love you too, Jo. Always have."

Her back arches gracefully as she comes apart beneath me, her inner walls pulsing around me so tightly that I can't hold back anymore. I follow her over the edge, her name torn from my lips as pleasure crashes through me in a tidal wave of ecstasy. I collapse on top of her, then roll over so she can lie on top of me. We're both breathing hard as I wrap my arms around her, holding her close like I'm afraid she might disappear. For a long moment, we simply lie here, hearts racing in tandem while the neon lights of Vegas paint patterns across our skin through the window.

"Well," Jo says eventually, her voice muffled against my neck, "I think we just set another record."

I chuckle, pressing a kiss to her hair. "Best eight seconds of my life, and that's saying something."

She lifts her head to look at me, eyes sparkling with mischief. "Only eight seconds? Cowboy, you're selling yourself short."

"Alright, maybe it was more like eight minutes," I concede, running my fingers through her tangled hair. "But who's counting?"

"I am," she says, settling more comfortably against me. "And I plan to keep very detailed records from now on."

The playful banter feels natural, easy in a way our relationship never has been before. No cameras, no contracts, no schemes—just us, genuinely devoted to each other.

I kiss her one more time, slowly, sensually. "So tell me Jolene, what do you want? Big ceremony, small gathering, elopement in Vegas while we're here? It's your call."

Jo's fingers trace the line of my jaw, her touch so tender that it makes my throat go thick. "I want something that feels like us. Not too fancy, not too plain. Somewhere with horses and family and the smell of hay in the air."

"The ranch," I suggest, picturing the oak tree by the creek where generations of McKendricks have carved their initials. "Just like we talked about before."

Her eyes light up. "Under that big oak tree with the mountains in the background. Simple, but perfect."

"Just like you."

She laughs, wrapping her legs around my waist. "Who knew Clay McKendrick was a smooth talker?"

"Only for you, darlin'."

Spending the rest of my life with this woman might be a life sentence, but it's one I'll gladly serve.

<h1 style="text-align:center;font-style:italic">Chapter Seventeen</h1>

Hearts and Home

The next morning, Jo and I are about to head out to the Las Vegas PRCA event when my fiancée stops us in the elevator—literally. She pushed the stop button and now pivots to face me. She's wringing her hands, her lips pursed.

I grasp her arms, bending my head to gaze into her eyes. "What's the matter, darlin'?"

Her gaze darts everywhere except to me until, finally, she rolls her shoulders back and lifts her chin, looking straight into my eyes. "I want you to meet my family, Clay. How would you feel about that?"

Stand here mute and rooted to this spot, unable to say a word. Her suggestion leaves me floored, kinda like the feeling I get right before the chute opens and I'm flung around by a bucking bull.

"Your family," I repeat slowly, studying her face. Jo's always been so self-contained, so independent. The fact that she wants me to meet her family feels like the biggest step we've taken yet.

She rushes ahead, unleashing a flurry of words. "I know it's complicated. They live in Colorado, which means we'd have to make a detour after Vegas. And I haven't exactly told them about us yet. I mean, they know about the engagement from the news, but they don't know it's real now, and my dad can be…Intimidating."

I cup her face, halting her nervous rambling with my thumb against her lips. "Jo, of course I want to meet your family. If I'm going to marry you, I should probably introduce myself to the people who raised such a stubborn, talented, beautiful woman."

The relief that washes over her face is adorable. Did she really think I'd say no?

"They're not like your family," she warns, leaning into my touch. "My dad…he's a legend in rodeo circles. Seven-time national champion. The great Hank Callahan."

I whistle low. "I know who your dad is, Jo. Everyone in rodeo knows Hank Callahan."

"That's the problem." She wriggles away, hitting the elevator button to get us moving again. "He casts a long shadow. And he has strong opinions about who his daughter should be with."

The elevator begins to descend, and I watch the numbers tick down, processing what she's telling me. Hank Callahan—the man's a living legend. Seriously, *a legend*. Seven national championships, more endorsement deals than any cowboy before or since, and a reputation for being tougher than a two-dollar steak. The fact that he's Jo's father explains a lot about her drive and perfectionism.

"What kind of strong opinions?" I ask, though I've got a sinking feeling I already know.

Jo scrunches up her face in a sheepish expression. "The kind that include Ivy League degrees and trust funds. Dad always figured I'd end up with someone from his social circle—another champion with a pedigree and connections. Not a struggling rancher from Montana."

The elevator dings as we reach the lobby, but neither of us moves when the doors slide open. I can see the doubt creeping back into her eyes, the same uncertainty that made her push me away that first night in Durango.

"Jo, look at me." I hold the door open with one hand while I tilt her chin up with the other. "I've faced down two-ton bulls with murder in their eyes. I think I can handle your dad."

A shaky smile tugs at her lips. "Bulls are predictable compared to Hank Callahan."

"Well then, I'll just have to be unpredictable right back." I wink at her as we finally exit the elevator. "Besides, I've got something those trust fund cowboys don't have."

"What's that?" Jo asks, falling into step beside me as we cross the glittering casino floor.

"I've got his daughter's heart." I clasp her hand, threading our fingers. "And I don't plan on giving it back. You're mine, Jolene, and I'm yours. It's a forever thing."

The blush that creeps up her cheeks is worth every ounce of nervousness I'm feeling about meeting rodeo royalty. We make our way through the casino toward the exit, and I can feel Jo's tension starting to ease with every step.

"You're pretty confident for a man who's about to face the most intimidating father in the Western United States," Jo says, but her grip on my hand tightens like she's drawing strength from the contact.

"Confident? Hell no. Terrified? Absolutely." I stop walking and turn to face her fully, right here in the middle of the casino with slot machines dinging around us. "But Jo, I'd face down a hundred Hank Callahans if it means proving to your family that I'm worthy of you."

Her gaze softens, and for a moment the vulnerability is back—that rare glimpse behind the armor she wears so well. "What if they don't think you're good enough? What if Dad takes one look at your bank statements and decides you're just another fortune hunter?"

I let out a short laugh, the sound echoing off the casino's high ceiling. "Then he'd be wrong. I've got my own ranch, my own career, and my own damn pride. I'm not after your money, Jo—I'm after you."

The conviction in my voice surprises even me. A month ago, I might've been worried about exactly what her father would think of my financial situation. Now, with the Western Heritage contract in my pocket and my future secured, I realize it doesn't matter what Hank Callahan thinks about my finances. All that matters is what he thinks about how I treat his daughter.

"Besides," I add, tugging her closer as a group of tourists stumble past us, "I seem to remember someone telling me that authentic always wins. If your dad's half the man you say he is, he'll see right through any bullshit and realize what's between us is genuine."

Jo's smile widens. "You honestly aren't scared of him, are you?"

"Nope." I guide her toward the exit again. "I've got a thicker skin than most people think. Thing is, I don't show it off for just anyone. Only mule-headed barrel racers."

She laughs. "Well then, you've picked the right woman."

The morning sun hits us like a spotlight as we walk outside, the Nevada heat already building despite the early hour. Our trailer is parked in the VIP section of the lot where Thunder and Jo's mare Blaze are both ready and waiting for today's events.

"So, that's a yes?" Jo asks as we cross the parking lot. "You'll come to Colorado after Vegas?"

I kiss her forehead. "Wild horses couldn't drag me away, darlin'."

"Speaking of wild horses…" Jo nods toward the arena in the distance, where we can see the stock trailers unloading. "We should probably focus on today's competition before we start worrying about family introductions."

"Good idea. What events are you entered in today?"

"Barrel racing and breakaway roping." Jo's voice takes on that familiar edge of competition. "And for you…"

"Bull riding and team roping." I grin at her. "Think we can sweep the board again?"

"With you? Always." She rises on her tiptoes to kiss my cheek. "But first, let's get these horses ready. Blaze gets cranky when she's kept waiting."

As we approach our trailer, I can see other competitors already warming up their mounts in the practice area. The familiar sounds of rodeo—horses nickering, leather creaking, gates swinging, and Buck's voice testing the PA system—settle over me like the arrival of an old friend. This world, with its dust and danger and pure adrenaline, has always been my sanctuary. Now, with Jo by my side, it feels like something more. It feels like home.

"Cranky horse or cranky father-in-law," I muse, lowering the trailer ramp. "Guess I'll be handling both soon enough."

Jo laughs, the sound bright and sweet. "At least Blaze can be bribed with sugar cubes. Dad's a bit more complicated."

Thunder greets me with a soft whicker as I enter the trailer, his dark eyes alert. The gelding seems to sense the importance of today, since he's practically dancing in place as I lead him down the ramp.

I stroke his neck. "Easy, boy. Save that energy for the arena."

"Thunder looks ready to run," Jo says, leading Blaze down the ramp beside us. Her mare tosses her head, equally eager for the day's events. "They must know something big's coming."

"Smart animals." I check Thunder's hooves before we start walking toward the warm-up arena. "Maybe they can sense that everything's changing."

Jo's eyes meet mine over the horses' backs. "Scared?"

"Of the competition? Never." I wiggle my eyebrows at her. "Of your dad? Terrified but ready."

She laughs, but there's a hint of nervousness in it. "Let's just focus on today. One challenge at a time."

"One challenge at a time," I echo, adjusting Thunder's bridle. "Wise words from a wise woman."

The Las Vegas sun beats down on us as we lead our horses toward the warm-up arena. Already, I can feel the familiar pre-competition excitement humming through my veins. But I also experience a new sense of purpose that goes beyond winning buckles or setting records.

Buck spots us from across the grounds and waves us over, grinning with all his laser-white teeth showing.

"There they are!" he declares, clapping me on the shoulder hard enough to make Thunder sidestep. "The golden couple of rodeo! Camera crew's already asking when you'll be available for some pre-event interviews."

Jo groans faintly beside me. "Can we at least warm up the horses first? Blaze needs a good twenty minutes or she'll be a nightmare in the arena."

I give her a squeeze and a quick kiss. "Absolutely. Take all the time you need, darlin'."

Chapter Eighteen
New Horizons

The Las Vegas event is incredible. I haven't even watched Jo doing her thing, and she hasn't seen me doing mine. We've been too excited about the rodeo and its unstoppable energy. But now, with my events finished and Thunder cooled down, I'm making my way to the barrel racing section to catch Jo's final run. The crowd's energy is infectious, and I can hear Buck revving up the arena as I push through the spectators.

"Next up, folks, we have the incomparable Jolene Callahan, riding Blaze!"

I find a spot along the rail just as Jo bursts out of the gate, and damn if she doesn't take my breath away every single time. Blaze moves like liquid fire beneath her, and Jo's body flows with the horse's rhythm in perfect harmony. She leans into the first barrel turn so low that her knee nearly kisses the dirt, but they clear it clean and tight.

"Look at that form!" Buck shouts. "Callahan's on pace for yet another record!"

The second barrel is even tighter. Blaze's hooves barely skim the ground as Jo guides the mare with nothing more than the slightest shift of weight and pressure from her legs. Jo and Blaze thunder toward the final barrel, and I find myself gripping the rail so hard my knuckles turn white.

"Come on, Jo," I whisper, though she can't possibly hear me over the noise.

She takes the final turn with surgical precision, Blaze's body curving around the barrel like they're part of the same organism. There's a moment—a fraction of a second—when I think they might clip it, but Jo shifts her weight just so, and they clear it by a whisper.

The race to the finish line is pure poetry. Jo's hair streams behind her like a battle flag as she gives Blaze her head, and the mare responds with an explosive burst of speed that has the crowd on their feet.

The timer flashes: 15.2 seconds. Another new arena record.

The deafening cheers of the crowd fill the arena, but all I can focus on is Jo's face as she brings Blaze to a sliding stop. Pure joy radiates from her like sunlight, and when her eyes find mine in the stands, grins and blows me a kiss. I do the same for her.

"Ladies and gentlemen," Buck exclaims with genuine awe, "that's not just an arena record—that's a Nevada state record! Jolene Callahan has just made rodeo history—again!"

I'm moving before I consciously decide to, vaulting over the rail and jogging toward the exit gate where Jo's walking Blaze in cool-down circles. She sees me coming and slides off her mare, rushing over to greet me.

"Did you see that?" she laughs, throwing her arms around my neck just as I reach her. "Did you see that last turn? I thought for sure we were going to clip it, but Blaze—God, she's incredible!"

"I saw every second of it, baby." I lift her off her feet and spin her around twice right here in the dirt. "You were perfect. Both of you."

She crushed her lips to mine. Our tongues tangle, and I grasp her ass while she mashes her body against me. When we break apart at last, she's still beaming, her cheeks flushed with excitement.

"Fifteen-point-two," she breathes against my lips. "I can't believe it."

"I never had any doubts." I set her down but keep my arms around her waist. "You've been building to this all season. That wasn't luck, darlin'—that was pure skill."

Blaze nudges my shoulder with her nose, and I reach up to stroke her velvety muzzle. "You too, girl. You're the best partner Jo could ask for."

Jo laughs, rubbing Blaze's neck affectionately. "We've got a pretty good team going, don't we? The four of us, I mean."

"The best team ever, darlin'."

Thunder's waiting back at the stables, probably wondering where his post-ride treat is. I make a mental note to stop by the concession stand for an apple on our way back.

"McKendrick! Callahan!" Buck's voice cuts through the crowd noise as he hustles toward us, his microphone still in his hand. "Get yourselves back in the arena, pronto! The sponsors want a photo with our record-breakers!"

Jo rolls her eyes, but her smile doesn't fade. "Duty calls. Ready for your closeup, cowboy?"

"As long as I'm standing beside you." I glance down at my dusty clothes. "Though I should probably clean up first. I look like I've been wrestling steers all day."

"You look gorgeous, Clay." She fluffs my hair with her fingertips. "Pure rugged cowboy with a touch of windblown sex appeal. The cameras will love it."

Buck's already herding us back toward the arena, chattering excitedly into his headset about photo opportunities and sponsor obligations. The crowd's still buzzing from Jo's record-breaking run, and I can see the Western Heritage Brands crew setting up their equipment near the winner's circle.

"There's our golden couple!" The campaign director, a sharp-dressed woman called Miranda, waves us over with the enthusiasm of someone who's just struck oil. "That run was absolutely perfect for our authentic western lifestyle brand!"

Jo handles the attention with her usual grace, answering questions about her technique and giving Blaze all the credit while cameras flash around us. I stand by her side, one hand resting on the small of her back. The subtle tension in her muscles that tells me she's starting to tire of the spotlight—for today. We've committed to whatever Western Heritage wants from us.

"Clay," Miranda coos, zeroing in on me, "we'd love to get some footage of you talking about watching Jo's record-breaking run. The devoted fiancé angle is pure gold."

"Happy to help." What I really want is to get Jo and our horses back to the stables, away from the spotlight. But I know this is part of the deal we've made—the visibility that's saving our careers and my family's ranch.

"Perfect! Just look at her like you were when she crossed that finish line," Miranda instructs, positioning me next to Jo while a cameraman adjusts his equipment.

I don't need any direction for that.

"That's it!" Miranda claps her hands. "Natural chemistry, people. This is what Western Heritage is all about!"

Jo catches my eye and gives me a tiny eye roll that only I can see. I squeeze her hand in silent understanding as we pose for what feels like the hundredth photo.

"Just a few more," Buck promises, reading our fatigue accurately. "Then you two can go take care of those horses and grab some well-deserved dinner."

The mention of food makes my stomach growl loud enough that Jo hears it over the crowd noise.

She grins at me and tries not to laugh, though she winds up spluttering. "Sounds like someone worked up an appetite watching me break records."

"Always do when I watch you ride," I reply, then realize how that sounds and feel my cheeks heat up. The reporters chuckle, scribbling notes, and Miranda seems positively delighted with the authentic banter.

"One more shot," the photographer calls out. "Can you two look at each other like you're sharing a secret?"

That's easy enough. We share plenty of secrets now—just between us. Like how Jo gets nervous before every run and hides it by meticulously checking Blaze's tack three times. Or how I still wake up some mornings surprised that this incredible woman chose me over all the smooth-talking cowboys with deeper pockets and shinier buckles.

The photographer snaps away as Jo leans closer, her voice barely a whisper meant only for me. "When we get back to the hotel tonight, I'm going to show you just how good breaking records makes me feel."

Whatever expression just crossed my face, it makes Miranda practically purr with satisfaction. "Wonderful! That's the shot we needed!"

Buck mercifully steps in before the heat building between Jo and me becomes obvious to everyone. "All right, folks, let's give our champions a chance to tend to their horses. Plenty more photo opportunities at tomorrow's events."

As the crowd disperses, Jo and I finally make our escape toward the stables. We lead our horses into the stable area, away from the chaos of cameras and crowds. Blaze is still prancing from leftover adrenaline, tossing her head like she knows she's just made history.

Jo pets the mare's neck while we walk. "Easy, girl. You've earned your oats tonight."

Thunder greets us with a low whicker from his stall, and I can see him eyeing the apple I grabbed from the concession stand on our way over. Smart horse. He knows the routine by now.

"How'd you do in the bull riding warm-ups?" Jo asks as she begins removing Blaze's tack.

"Incredible. I survived the toughest bull out there and took first in the preliminary round." I hand Thunder his apple and start working on his bridle. "Eighty-seven points on Diablo's Fury. Buck nearly fell out of the announcer's booth."

"Seems like we're both on fire today."

I hang Thunder's bridle on the hook outside his stall. "Must be something in the Nevada air. Or maybe it's just knowing we've finally got our lives figured out."

For the first time ever, I can speak those words without a trace of irony or regret. Jolene Callahan saved me from a lonely life, and I will always be grateful for that.

Chapter Nineteen

Going Home, Pt. 1

Not sure what kind of greeting I expected to receive once we arrived at the ranch owned by the Callahans. But it definitely wasn't a passel of men, women and children descending on us both. Jo takes it all in stride, naturally. These are her people, after all. I assumed they'd be slightly suspicious of me, considering that they had never met or spoken to me until today.

I was wrong on that account too.

"Well, look what our Jo-Jo brought home!" Those words came from a woman who's clearly Jo's mother. She has the same auburn hair and emerald eyes. And she wraps me in a suffocating hug before I can even get my bearings. "You must be the famous fiancé we've been hearing absolutely nothing about."

Jo stands beside me, clearing her throat. "Mom, this is—"

"Sweet girl, we know exactly who this is," declares an older man with a wrinkled face and kind eyes. The guy strides up to me, his posture confident, and extends his hand. "Been following your career for years now, son. Hell of a ride you had in Deadwood last month."

I shake his hand, trying not to look as confused as I feel. These people are treating me like family, and I've been on their property for all of two minutes. Back home, it takes at least three generations and a blood oath to get this kind of welcome. "Thank you, sir. I appreciate that."

"Sir?" Jo's mother laughs, and it sounds identical to her daughter's laughter when she's genuinely amused rather than putting on that polished pageant smile. "Honey, you're practically family now. Call me Mae, and this old goat is Hank, my big strong honeybun."

"Old goat?" Frank shakes his head slightly, though he's grinning. "Mae, give the boy some breathing room. He looks like he's about to bolt."

"I'm fine," I lie, because the truth is I do feel like bolting. Not because of Jo's parents. It's because I see even more people pouring out of the house, the barns, and the pasture out back.

A younger woman who looks a lot like Jo sidles up to me, wearing a knowing grin. "So tell me, mystery man, how exactly did our Jo manage to keep you secret for so long? She's terrible at keeping her mouth shut about anything important. I'm Jolene's baby sister, by the way."

Jo sets her hands on her hips. "I am standing right here, Casey. And you jabber so loud nobody could possibly miss anything you say."

"I'm talking to the hottie, not you."

"His name is Clay McKendrick, not 'the hottie.' What, have you regressed to being twelve years old?"

"Ooh, must be true love if Jo-Jo's this protective of you, Clay." Casey winks at me. "You look like the type who might actually give us some straight answers."

I smile awkwardly, feeling like I'm in a spotlight I never auditioned for—with a sassy girl calling the shots. "I'm not sure what answers I'm supposed to have, to be honest."

"Like how you two met?" Casey prompts, sidling closer. "Or when you decided to get hitched? Or why we're only meeting you now when the wedding's supposedly right around the corner?"

"Casey," Jo warns, her voice dropping to a dangerously low octave while she squints at her sister.

I clear my throat and offer up the vaguest answer. "Well, when you know it's right, you just…know."

"That's right," Mae chimes in, looping her arm through mine and steering me toward the house. "Love doesn't always follow a timeline. Now come on in, Clay. I've got fresh lemonade and a peach cobbler that's still warm from the oven."

My stomach growls just thinking about food. And peach cobbler? *Mm-mm-mm.* My mouth is already watering.

Before I can protest, I'm being swept along by Mae's enthusiastic hospitality. Jo trails behind us, throwing me an apologetic smile and mouthing the words, "Sorry."

As we walk inside, the scents of cinnamon and other savory delights fill my nostrils. My stomach growls again.

"You hungry, son?" Hank asks, appearing at my other elbow. "Mae's been cooking all morning, ever since Jo called to say she was bringing you by."

"You didn't have to go to any trouble, sir." Ranch food back home is beans, beef, and whatever vegetables survive our temperamental growing season.

"Trouble?" Mae laughs again and kisses my cheek. "Honey, feeding people is what we do. Besides, I've been dying to meet the man who finally caught our Jo's eye. Sit, Clay, sit!"

She gestures to a large wooden table surrounded by mismatched chairs, each one worn by time and maintained with love.

Jo huffs. "Ma, please don't talk to Clay like he's a farm dog."

"When did I do that, Jo-Jo?"

"Just now. You told him 'sit, Clay, sit.'"

Mae waves away Jo's complaint. "Oh, hogwash. Clay knew what I meant, didn't you?"

"Sure did."

I do like Mae told me to, and Jo slips into the chair beside me, her knee brushing mine under the table. That small point of contact shouldn't feel as reassuring as it does. My head seems to be spinning, but I think that's just confusion. I never got the chance to prepare for this meeting, and after what Jo said about her father, I'm a little confused. Hank has been pleasant to me. The ogre Jo described is nowhere in sight.

"So, Clay," Hank says, settling onto a chair across from us while Mae bustles around the kitchen, "Jo tells us you've got a spread up north?"

"Yes, sir—I mean, Hank." The formality slips out automatically. "McKendrick Ranch. Been in my family for generations."

Casey plops down on my other side, still eyeing me like I'm a puzzle she's determined to solve. "And you met our Jo-Jo at…"

"The Tampa Rodeo last year," I explain. "She was competing in barrel racing, and I was in the bronc and bull riding events."

"Ooooh, love at first ride," Casey teases, wiggling her eyebrows.

Jo shoots her sister a withering look. "It wasn't quite that simple."

"Never is with Jo," a deep voice adds as a tall man who could only be Jo's brother enters the kitchen. He extends his hand to me. "I'm Levi, the oldest Callahan kid and chief wrangler of this bunch of yahoos."

Jo feigns a scowl. "Speak for yourself."

Mae sets a glass of lemonade in front of me. I take my first sip, and I'm hit with a flavor so sweet it could probably dissolve a tooth on contact. "Jo was absolutely determined to stay single forever after that horrible business with—"

"Mom," Jo interrupts. "Can we not talk about Tyler? My ex-husband is off limits at family gatherings, remember?"

"Sorry, honey, I figured Clay ought to know."

Right then, a dozen or so more people start showing up—cousins, aunts, uncles, and what looks like half the county filing through the front door like they've been summoned by some invisible dinner bell. My eyes widen as the kitchen fills to capacity, and even more folks gather in the halls and living areas and who knows where else.

I give my fiancée a sideways glance, raising my brows briefly.

Her face cinches up, and she lifts her shoulders, spreading her hands in a "sorry" gesture.

I pat her thigh, smiling so she'll know I'm not upset.

"Word travels fast around here," Jo hisses under her breath. "It's not usually like this, but everybody's thrilled to meet you."

"Clay McKendrick!" booms a voice from the doorway. A barrel-chested man with silver hair pushes through the crowd. "I'll be damned. Watched you ride that devil bull in San Antonio two years back. Thought for sure you were gonna end up eating dirt, but you hung on."

I stand up to shake his hand, grateful for familiar territory. "Thank you, sir, I remember meeting you in San Antonio. That bull was Widow Maker. Nearly broke my ribs, but it was worth it for the score."

"Uncle Pete runs the feed store in town," Jo explains quickly. "He thinks he knows everything about everybody's business."

"Damn right I do!" Uncle Pete slaps me on the back—hard. "Boy, you got yourself a real firecracker there. Jo's been breaking hearts and taking names since she was old enough to date."

"I have not been breaking hearts," Jo protests, her nostrils flaring like a bull's.

"What about that Henderson boy? And the preacher's son? And—"

"Uncle Pete, I swear I will put salt in your coffee tomorrow morning if you don't hush your mouth."

The old man chuckles and settles into a chair that creaks under his weight. "She's feisty, this one. You gonna be able to handle her, son?"

I glance at Jo, who's glaring at her uncle like she's plotting his demise. "I'm learning that handling Jo isn't as difficult as I expected."

She smacks my thigh, but her eyes glitter with humor.

More introductions follow in rapid succession. There's Aunt Birdie who insists on pinching my cheeks, Cousin Ray who wants to arm wrestle, and at least six kids whose names I lose track of immediately. Every single person seems genuinely excited to meet me, which only makes the knot in my stomach tighten further.

"Alright, everybody, give the man some air!" Mae calls out, wielding a wooden spoon like a weapon. "Clay's not going anywhere, so you can all get your turns to interrogate him later. Right now, we're gonna eat."

The food is amazing, and the company is even better. We wind up dining outside where the Callahan clan sets up enough picnic tables to serve the entire United States Army. I learn that Jo's brother served in the Air Force for ten years, and that a distant cousin became a congressman.

Holy cow, this family is incredible.

After two more days with the Callahans, Jo and I say our goodbyes and drive straight to Montana and the McKendrick ranch. I've been looking forward to seeing my family again, and I can't wait to introduce them to Jolene.

Chapter Twenty

Going Home, Pt. 2

The Montana landscape unfolds around us in undulating waves of green and gold, and rolling hills unfurl toward the jagged mountains. Jo's been quiet for the last hour, her fingers tapping a nervous rhythm against her thigh. I never would've believed she could get this anxious.

"You okay over there?" I ask, glancing sideways at her.

"Just peachy," she says, but her voice has that tight quality that tells me she's lying. "I'm about to meet the family of my formerly fake fiancé. Does your family know about the sham relationship?"

"No. I would never tell them without your permission. But since your family knows now…"

She covers her face and groans pitifully. "What if they hate me for what I convinced you to do?"

"When we told your gigantic family, none of them cared. Your dad didn't pummel me until I bled, and he never even issued scary threats."

"That's not comforting, Clay."

I chuckle, keeping my eyes on the winding road. "Nobody's gonna bite you or scratch your eyes out. Well, except maybe Grandma Esther, but she only does that when she's feeling ornery."

"Clay!" Jo's eyes bulge.

"I'm kidding, darlin'." I reach over to squeeze her hand. "Everyone will fall for you on sight—just like I did."

Jo's lips curl into a reluctant smile as she grips my free hand with all the strength of a dog with a bone. "I didn't think Clay McKendrick did falling."

"Never had until I met you." I lift her hand to kiss the knuckles. "Now, I keep falling over and over every time you smile at me."

Jo rubs her cheek on my shoulder. "Same for me." She turns her face toward the window. "Your sister knows the truth, right? About how this all started?"

"Sarah knows we weren't exactly planning on forever when we first got engaged," I hedge, taking the turn onto the long gravel drive that leads to the ranch. "But she doesn't know all the details. Most everybody has heard about it already, thanks to the tabloids."

"I'm so sorry, Clay. I know I'm acting like a crazy person."

"Unless you start foaming at the mouth, you are not crazy."

The McKendrick Ranch sign comes into view, weathered and familiar against the big sky. My throat constricts, partly because I haven't been home in such a long time and partly because I can't wait to share my love for Jo with my family. While we bump along the familiar ruts in the gravel, I catalog every little thing—from wildflowers to clouds. I'm home. Even after all these years on the circuit, this place still feels like the center of my universe.

Jo sits up straighter, her hand gripping my thigh. "Oh my God, Clay. It's even more beautiful than I remember."

The main building sprawls ahead of us, a two-story farmhouse with a wraparound porch that's seen more family gatherings than I can count. The barn sits off to the left, its red paint faded but not erased. Beyond that, the pastures stretch toward the mountains where our cattle graze in lazy clusters.

"Wait until you see it at sunset," I tell her, pulling up next to the porch steps. "The whole sky turns purple and orange, and—"

The front door bangs open, and my sister Sarah bursts out, practically vaulting over the porch railing in her excitement.

"They're here!" she hollers back into the house before racing toward my truck.

I barely have time to put the vehicle in park before Sarah yanks open my door.

"Move your butt, big brother," she demands, shoving at my shoulder. "I've been dying to talk to Jo."

My fiancée grins.

Sarah has that effect on a lot of people. She's eternally cheerful.

Mom and Dad make their way out of the house, though Dad still needs a bit of help getting up and down steps, stairs, and other sorts of inclines. His knee surgery was supposed to fix things, but he's still recovering. Mom hovers near him, one hand discreetly at his elbow while pretending she's not helping at all.

"I'm moving as fast as I can," Dad shouts to Sarah. "Some of us don't have springs for legs."

"Clay!" Mom hollers, waving enthusiastically. Her salt-and-pepper hair is pulled back in its usual practical bun, and she's wearing the apron I got her for Christmas three years ago. "Bring that girl of yours up here so I can give her a proper hug!"

Dad smirks. "That means she wants to suffocate her."

Mom shakes her head, though it's an affectionate expression.

"Clay!" Sarah practically drags me out of the truck, wrapping her arms around my midsection in a fierce hug. "You've been gone way too long."

"It's only been a couple months, squirt." I ruffle her hair, something she hates, and she predictably swats at my hand.

"I'm twenty-four, not twelve," she reminds me, but her mock scowl dissolves into another grin when she spots Jo climbing out of the passenger side. "Jo! I'm so glad you're finally here!"

Jo barely has time to close the truck door before Sarah engulfs her in a hug that would put a grizzly to shame. To her credit, Jo returns the embrace with just as much enthusiasm, her nervousness seemingly forgotten in the face of Sarah's boundless energy.

"I've been texting her non-stop," Sarah explains to me over Jo's shoulder. "We're practically besties now."

I raise an eyebrow at Jo, who shrugs and mouths, "She's persistent."

"Let the poor girl breathe, pumpkin," Dad calls out from the porch, his voice gruff but warm. "You're worse than a barn cat with a new litter, Sarah."

The youngest McKendrick reluctantly releases Jo but immediately links their arms together. "Come on, I'll give you the grand tour while

Clay deals with the bags. Mom's been cooking since dawn—hope you're hungry!"

"Starving," Jo says, allowing herself to be led toward the house.

As I watch them go, I feel a strange mix of relief and apprehension swirling inside me. Sarah's clearly taken to Jo like a duck to water, which is exactly what I hoped for. But now comes the real test—Mom and Dad.

"You gonna stand there gawking all day, or are you coming up here to greet your old man?" Dad hollers, though there's no real irritation in his voice.

I grab our bags from the truck bed and jog up the porch steps. Dad's waiting with his arms open, and I set the luggage down to give him a careful hug, mindful of his still-healing knee.

"Good to have you home, son." He claps me on the back, and I swear I detect tears gathering in his eyes. He wipes them away quickly, returning to his usual gruffly kind demeanor. "Been too quiet around here without you stirring up trouble."

"I never stirred up trouble, Dad. That's pure propaganda."

He raises his brows. "What about that motorcycle you bought with the money you earned from mopping floors in the hardware store? It was so loud I could hear it from our front porch, ten miles away."

Mom appears at my elbow, not waiting for an invitation before pulling me into a fierce hug. "Oh, my sweet boy, you look too thin. Have you been eating?"

"Yes, Mom," I say automatically. It doesn't matter that I'm thirty-two years old and have been feeding myself successfully ever since I turned eighteen. She'll always think I'm starving.

Her gaze flicks toward the house where Sarah has already ushered Jo inside. And Mom pats my cheek. "Your girl is the prettiest thing I've ever seen, sweetie. Those tabloid photos didn't do her justice. But I'm so happy you finally found the right woman, Clay."

"Thanks, Mom."

She dusts off her apron. "Time for dinner. Then you and Jo will want to get some rest after your long road trip to get here. We assumed you two would share a bed."

"Yeah, Mom, we will."

As always, the meal Mom whips up is homemade, homegrown, and absolutely delicious. Meryl McKendrick knows how to feed her family—and a passel of guests too. Tonight, however, it's just me, my parents, my sister, and Grandma Esther. Grandpa passed away fifteen years ago, but becoming a widow hadn't toned down her feisty nature.

The woman of the house sits at the head of the table, her silver hair pinned in a perfect chignon. Despite being ninety-three years old, Grandma Esther still serves as the head of the household. Her sharp blue eyes—the same shade as mine—take in every detail of Jo's appearance and mannerisms with the precision of a hawk sizing up prey.

"So, my dear," Grandma Esther begins, setting her fork down with deliberate care, "you're the barrel racer who stole my grandson's heart."

Jo straightens in her chair, meeting Grandma's gaze head-on. "Yes, ma'am. Though I'd argue Clay stole my heart first."

Sarah snorts, trying not to laugh, while Dad coughs to cover a chuckle. Mom shoots them both warning looks, but I notice the corner of her mouth twitching.

Grandma Esther remains impassive for a moment, then she breaks into an impish smile. "I like this one, Clay. She's got gumption."

"Thank you, Mrs. McKendrick."

"Call me Esther, dear. Or Grandma, since you'll be family soon enough." She winks at me before turning her attention back to Jo. "Now tell me, how many championships have you won? Clay mentioned you're quite the accomplished rider."

Jo launches into a modest recounting of her career highlights while I watch my family lean toward Jo, completely captivated by her tales. Sarah peppers her with questions about training techniques, Mom wants to know about her favorite horses, and Dad nods approvingly when Jo mentions her dedication to proper animal care. When Jo and I finally get to our room, we're so tired that all we want to do is undress and go to sleep.

The next day, we meet with the Western Heritage folks in Laramie to map out a year-long plan for our reality show. It's really happening. Jo and I are about to become celebrities.

Chapter Twenty-One
The Reality Show

O uch!" Jo exclaims as I leap up, about to rush past the partition that separates us. "Jo, are you hurt? I can get a doctor or a medic or something."

"No, Clay, that's unnecessary. The young woman fitting my dress accidentally pricked me." I hear small sobs, and Jo shushing the girl. "Relax, Nora, you didn't mean to do it. I'm fine."

"Are you sure?" Those words are followed by a sniffle.

"Positive. Let's keep going."

I'm watching from the other side of the boutique dress shop while my fiancée is getting fitted for the dress I'm not allowed to see—until the wedding, that is. Once we tie the knot, nothing will stand between us ever again.

She'll be mine, and I'll be hers, forever.

Wedding. The word echoes in my mind, and I get a strange feeling in my chest every time I think about that. I never imagined I'd be standing in a bridal boutique while Jo gets fitted for her dream gown.

"Mr. McKendrick, would you like something to drink while you wait?" The boutique owner approaches me, wearing a practiced smile. "Champagne, perhaps? It's complimentary for the groom."

"Just water, thanks," I reply, shifting uncomfortably in the plush velvet chair they've designated as the "groom spot."

Jo's parents are footing the bill for everything. They know my folks could never gather enough dough to do that. Our moms offered to organize the whole event. But Jo and I assured them that isn't necessary. Only then did Meryl and May admit this mega event was a bit much for them to organize, anyway.

Jo peeks around the partition from her perch on the pedestal I'd spied when the wedding planner had put it up earlier. Jo gives me that look—the one that says I'm being too serious again. She's right. I can't help feeling uncomfortable, but I need to relax for Jo's sake.

The shop owner is about to walk away.

"Actually, champagne sounds perfect." I announce. "Might as well celebrate."

Jo grins. "That's a great idea, Clay. Save some bubbly for me."

"Will do."

I already have my tux—a designer number that Jo swears will make me the best-dressed groom ever in the history of rodeo. But we'll both become something much worse. We're about to begin our careers in reality television, rodeo style. Miranda had sweet-talked us into making the wedding a part of the show, and actually, we've been looking forward to beginning two new chapters in our lives—marriage and fame. Not sure anybody outside of the rodeo circuit will care about the lives of a cowboy and a barrel racer. But Miranda swears the world is hungry for authentic rodeo romance.

"Trust me," she'd said last week over coffee, while she showed us audience demographics and ratings projections on her tablet. "People want the dust and the glory and the love story beneath it all."

My mind reels back to the present as the shop owner returns with two flutes of champagne. She hands one to me, and I take the other around the partition to Jo without peeking. I hear her giggle, followed by Nora's relieved laughter. At least someone's relaxed now.

I take a sip and let the bubbles dance on my tongue. Not bad for a guy who usually sticks to beer after a long day at the ranch.

"How's it looking back there, Jo?" With all my willpower, I resist the urge to peek. Mom would have my hide if I broke tradition, and the PRCA boys would never let me hear the end of it.

"Almost done, Clay!" she confirms cheerfully. "You're going to flip when you see this dress. It's divine. Like something out of a fairy tale."

I smile, leaning against the wall beside the partition. "I bet *you* make the dress look good, not the other way around."

The boutique owner passes by with an approving nod. I can hear the quiet murmurs of Nora and Jo discussing final adjustments. This whole wedding business still feels surreal. For months, I was focused solely on making it through the circuit, keeping the ranch afloat, and helping pay for Dad's medical bills. Winning some events was a bonus. But now I'm standing in a fancy boutique while a camera crew waits outside to capture our "authentic rodeo romance" the minute we step onto the sidewalk.

"Mr. McKendrick," the boutique owner says, returning with a small plate of fancy-looking cookies. "Some refreshments while you wait."

I take one cookie to be polite. "Thanks. How much longer will this take?"

Jo emerges from behind the partition, beaming at me so brightly that it wouldn't surprise me to see a glowing halo above her head. I jump up from my chair and can't resist teasing her a little bit. "You're wearing jeans and a denim shirt for the wedding? I thought you were dead set on a fancy gown."

Jo rolls her eyes, but she can't hide her smile. "You're hilarious, Clay. And I'd marry you in jeans and boots if that's what it came to."

"We could save your parents a fortune that way." I offer her the champagne flute.

"Don't you dare," the boutique owner gasps, clearly horrified at the thought. "This dress is an absolute masterpiece."

Jo takes a sip of champagne, her eyes meeting mine over the rim of the glass. There's something in that look that makes my heart skip—a mix of mischief and sweetness that's uniquely Jo.

"All done for today, Ms. Callahan," Nora says, emerging with pin-pricked fingers but seeming much calmer. "We'll have the final alterations ready next week."

As we walk out of the boutique, a crowd of reporters clamor to get a good shot and write down anything we might say. Jo and I pose for pictures, but otherwise, we wave off any questions. The camera crew maintains a polite distance from us and the reporters.

"No spoilers about the dress!" Jo calls out as we make our way through the throng. She grips my hand tightly, pulling me toward the black SUV that's waiting at the curb. Miranda insisted on providing transportation—another perk of our new "celebrity status." But I still don't feel famous. I'm just a cowboy who loves rodeos.

"They act like we're genuinely famous," I grumble, helping Jo into the vehicle before sliding in beside her.

"Well, cowboy, better get used to it." She leans her head against my shoulder, snuggling up to me. "I saw the rough cut of the first episode last night. Miranda says our social media following has already tripled."

The driver pulls away from the curb, leaving the small crowd of entertainment reporters behind.

I wrap my arm around Jo's shoulders, feeling her body relax. "Was it weird? Seeing yourself on TV, I mean?"

"Completely bizarre. But you look darn good on camera." Jo pokes my ribs. "All rugged and mysterious. The camera loves those blue eyes of yours."

I ignore her comment about my eyes. It's…weird. "I'm confused half the time, and ready to elope with you in the dead of night the rest of the time."

"That's part of your charm." Jo sits up and turns to face me, tucking one leg beneath her. "Clay, are you having second thoughts about all this? The cameras, the show, the publicity?"

I consider her question while watching the Colorado countryside roll past the tinted windows. "About marrying you? Never. About turning our lives into entertainment?" I pause, choosing my words carefully. "Sometimes I wonder if we're making a deal with the devil."

"Miranda's hardly the devil. More like a very determined business-woman in designer cowboy boots."

"You know what I mean, Jo. Once this airs, our lives won't be private anymore. Every fight, every kiss, every time I mess up—it'll be out there for everyone to see."

Jo folds her hands around mine. "Is that what's really bothering you? That people might see you mess up?"

I shift uncomfortably in the leather seat. She knows me too well. "Maybe. Hell, I don't know. Yesterday I was just Clay McKendrick, an un-known cowboy trying to keep his family's ranch from going under. Now I'm supposed to be this romantic hero for millions of viewers."

"You've always been my romantic hero. That hasn't changed."

The SUV hits a pothole, jostling us both. Through the partition, I can hear our driver offering an apology, though his words are muffled.

"What if they don't like us, Jo?" The words slip out before I can stop them. "What if we're boring? What if—"

She squeezes my hand, cutting off my spiral of doubt. "Then we'll be boring together. And we'll still be getting married, and I'll still love you, and we'll still have the ranch." Her green eyes hold mine with that unwavering confidence I've always admired. "The show is just a means to an end, Clay. It's not the sum total of our lives."

"Are you positive you want to run the McKendrick ranch with me? It's way up there in Montana. Your folks are in Colorado."

Her cheeks dimple, and her eyes sparkle. "I've heard about this weird metal contraption called an airplane that can take you to almost anywhere in the world..."

"You're hilarious, Jo."

"Cheered you up, didn't I?" She kisses my cheek. "Remember what I said."

I pull her closer. "The show is just a means to an end. It's not who we are."

I exhale slowly, and some of the tension melts away. "When did you get so wise?"

"I've always been the Yoda of the West. You were just too busy staring at my ass to notice." She winks, and I can't help but laugh.

The SUV slows as we approach the turnoff to the McKendrick ranch. I'm home. The place looks a little different—a little better—since the first check from the network cleared. New paint on the barn, repaired fencing, and Dad's medical bills paid up through next year. That alone makes this whole reality TV circus worth it.

"Speaking of your ass..." I let my hand drift lower on her back as I whisper in her ear, "Been too long since we knocked boots. Could we sneak away to that place I showed you? The one at the far end of the acreage."

Her lips form a knowing smile. "Two smart people like us can make that happen for sure."

But right now, it's time to paste on our professional smiles and give the press what they want.

Chapter Twenty-Two

Making It Real

After two months as reality stars, Jo and I declared that we need a break to rest and refresh ourselves. We never did get around to that naughty interlude on the far side of the ranch. Today, we're in the kitchen at Jo's family homestead—about to show off our cooking skills for the Callahans. A passel of relatives and neighbors have lined up outside to watch our show live on a movie-theater size screen.

Jo adjusts her apron—a frilly pink monstrosity that clashes spectacularly with her usual no-nonsense style—and shoots me a look that could melt steel.

"I still can't believe you agreed to this cooking challenge, Clay." She ties the apron strings with more ferocity than seems necessary. I swear her nostrils flared too, and her gaze has gone flinty.

"Hey, you're the one who said we needed good publicity after that unfortunate incident with the mechanical bull," I remind her, pulling on my own apron. Mine's got little cowboys printed all over it, which somehow makes me feel less masculine.

The cameras are already rolling, and I can hear the crowd outside whooping it up. Mrs. Callahan insisted on turning this into a proper neighborhood event, complete with betting pools on whether we'll burn down the kitchen or actually produce something edible.

"Welcome back to 'Roping Hearts'," our host announces. Her blindingly white smile borders on being radioactive under the kitchen lights. "I'm, Daphne Clark. And today we're visiting the gorgeous Callahan family ranch where our lovebirds will be attempting to cook a sumptuous meal for Jo's family and neighbors right here in Colorado!"

Jo's jaw clenches, and I can practically feel the waves of irritation rolling off her. She hates being called a lovebird almost as much as she hates that ridiculous apron.

"So, what's on the menu today?" our host continues, gesturing dramatically at the ingredients spread across the massive farmhouse table. It's a prop, of course. The Callahan's kitchen table wasn't rustic enough, according to Daphne.

"Chicken fried steak, mashed potatoes, and green beans," Jo says, her TV smile firmly in place despite the murder in her eyes. Our contract never mentioned cooking. "It's a family recipe, Daphne."

I lean against the counter, trying to seem casual while, internally, I'm panicking. The closest I've come to cooking chicken fried steak was ordering it at truck stops. But Jo doesn't know that, and I intend to keep it that way. She's already annoyed enough with me after I accidentally volunteered us for this culinary spectacle.

"Family recipe, huh?" I whisper as Daphne moves to interview Jo's grandmother about the dish's heritage. "You didn't mention that part."

"Because it wasn't relevant until you got us into this mess," Jo hisses back through her clenched teeth, her smile never faltering for the cameras. "Just follow my lead and try not to set anything on fire."

"I resent that implication." But my confidence wavers when Jo hands me a meat mallet. "What exactly am I supposed to do with this?"

"Tenderize the steak, cowboy." She smirks, clearly enjoying my discomfort. "Unless that's too complicated for your pretty little head to fathom."

I growl under my breath. Seriously, I do. Then I take the mallet, weighing it in my hand like it's a foreign object that mysteriously landed in the kitchen. "I'll have you know I've handled plenty of tools in my day."

"Is that right?" Jo arches an eyebrow, her sarcastic expression somehow turning me on. This is foreplay for us these days.

"Watch and learn, Rodeo Queen." I position the meat on the cutting board and bring the mallet down with more force than necessary. The resulting *thwack* echoes through the kitchen, and a piece of raw steak flies off the counter.

Daphne's cameraman zooms in just as I scramble to retrieve the steak from the floor.

"Five-second rule?" I offer, shrugging my shoulders.

Jo rolls her eyes but there's a hint of amusement there. "Not on national television, genius." She slides a fresh piece of steak my way. "Try again. Gently this time."

I approach the meat cautiously while Jo efficiently dices onions, her knife moving in a practiced rhythm that makes me feel even more incompetent. She's clearly done this a thousand times, while I'm over here treating a piece of beef like it might explode.

"You know," I mutter, giving the steak another tentative tap, "this would be easier if you'd mentioned your grandmother was watching."

Through the window, I can see Grandma Callahan perched in her lawn chair, arms crossed, studying my technique with the intensity of a rodeo judge. Her expression suggests she's already marked me down several points.

"Scared of a little old lady?" Jo's knife never pauses as she speaks, and bits of onion transform into perfectly uniform pieces.

I squint at Jo. "That 'little old lady' looks like she could take me in a fair fight."

"She probably could." Jo dumps the onions into a cast-iron skillet that's older than both of us combined. The sizzle fills the kitchen with a sound that makes my stomach growl. "Grandma Callahan didn't raise five kids and run a ranch for sixty years by being gentle."

"Great. So when I mess this up, she'll probably challenge me to a duel."

"Nah, she'll just tell everyone at church that you're useless in the kitchen." Jo glances over at my pathetic attempt at tenderizing meat. "Which, based on current evidence, wouldn't be a lie."

Daphne materializes beside us with that smile TV hosts perfect for maximum drama. "How are our lovebirds doing? Any kitchen chemistry brewing?"

I nearly choke on my own spit. Jo's cheeks flush pink, but she recovers faster than I do.

"Oh, there's definitely something brewing," she says sweetly, then leans closer to me. "Mostly disaster."

The cameraman chuckles, and I force a laugh. "She's just mad because I'm about to show her up with my superior culinary skills."

"Superior?" Jo's voice goes up an octave. "You just asked me if we needed to wash the potatoes before peeling them."

"It was a legitimate question!"

"Of course you wash them, Clay. Who wants to eat dirty food?"

Daphne's eyes light up like it's Christmas morning. Bickering is reality TV gold, apparently. "Tell us, Jo, what's it like cooking with your fiancé? Any secrets to making it work?"

Jo's smile could cut glass. "Communication is key. For instance, I communicate that he should stay out of my way, and he communicates his complete incompetence through interpretive kitchen disasters."

I smack my mallet down on the counter. "Hey now—"

"Remember the pancake incident?"

"I thought we agreed never to speak of the pancake incident again," I snarl, giving the steak another whack. I'm probably veering into culinary assault territory. "In my defense, I didn't know pancake batter could actually catch fire."

"And yet, somehow, you managed to do just that." Jo's hands move with practiced efficiency as she prepares the egg wash. "Just like you managed to get us into this cooking challenge when you know perfectly well the only thing you can make is reservations."

I smack the mallet down on the counter even harder than before.

Daphne leans in, virtually salivating at our bickering. "So, there's trouble in paradise? Tension in the kitchen often reflects tension in the relationship, doesn't it?"

"The only tension here," I say, forcing another smile, "is between this steak and my mallet. Got it?"

Daphne backs away, hands raised in surrender, but the gleam in her eyes tells me she's got what she wanted. More drama for the highlight reel.

"You're doing it wrong," Jo whispers once the host is out of earshot. She covers her hand with mine on the mallet. The sudden warmth of her touch has the odd effect of making me horny. "Like this, Clay. Firm but controlled."

I clear my throat. "I knew that."

"Sure you did, cowboy." There's a hint of affection beneath the sarcasm that proves Jo has been playing it up for the camera. While she guides my hand in a rhythmic pattern across the meat, I struggle to control myself and not think about how her body is pressed against mine or how her breath tickles my ear.

Through the window, I catch Grandma Callahan nodding approvingly, though whether it's about my tenderizing technique or Jo's proximity to me, I can't tell.

"All right, steak's ready," I pronounce, shuffling backward before I do something stupid like kiss her neck on national television. Then again, Miranda and Daphne would probably love that.

"Finally, Clay. What took so long?" Jo dips the meat into flour, then egg wash, then more flour with movements so smooth they could be choreographed. "Now comes the fun part."

She heats butter in a massive cast-iron skillet, and when it's shimmering, she slides the first piece of steak in. The sizzle is immediate and aggressive, sending up a cloud of steam that makes the kitchen smell like heaven.

I reach for the next piece. "My turn."

"Absolutely not." Jo blocks me with her hip, which does nothing to help my concentration. "You'll splash melted butter everywhere and probably burn yourself."

Suddenly, I get a fantastic idea. So, I shuffle closer to Jo and whisper into her ear, "Let's give these people a real comedy routine."

Her lips curve into a mischievous smile, and she nods her approval.

With a wink, I reach around Jo to grab the next piece of steak, intentionally pressing against her back. Then I announce too loudly, "I think I've got this part handled, darlin'!"

"Clay McKendrick, I swear to—" Jo starts, but I've already dropped the steak into the melted butter with a dramatic flourish.

It splatters everywhere. A tiny droplet lands on my forearm, and I yelp like I've been shot, doing an exaggerated dance around the kitchen while shaking my arm.

"My hero," Jo deadpans, flipping the first steak with perfect precision. "Ladies and gentlemen, meet the man who survived being thrown from a bull but can't handle a little hot melted butter."

The crowd outside roars with laughter. I catch a glimpse of Grandma Callahan shaking her head, but there's definitely a smile tugging at her lips.

Maybe this reality show thing won't be an unbearable nightmare after all.

Chapter Twenty-Three
Going Off the Grid

Six days after our culinary debacle at the Callahan ranch, Jo and I demanded some time off from the craziness. Three days, that's all we want. Three days without cameras, reporters, or even our families around us. Miranda, our producer, tried to argue, of course. She babbled on and on about "momentum" and "viewer engagement metrics" until Jo threatened to walk away from the whole show. I've never seen Miranda backpedal so fast.

It took me ten minutes to settle Jo down. Only then did Miranda finally consent to our little vacation—with no one watching us.

So now we're heading to a little cabin that belongs to one of Jo's cousins. It's tucked away in the Montana Mountains where cell service is spotty at best and the nearest neighbor is five miles down a dirt road. Sounds like paradise to me.

"Turn left up here," Jo says, pointing to a barely visible path between the pines. Her hair is loose today, flowing over her shoulders instead of in its usual practical ponytail. It's a good look on her.

She's also in charge of the map her cousin gave us.

Following Jo's instructions, I guide our truck onto what can only generously be called a road. "You're sure this is right? Looks like we're driving straight into the wilderness."

"That's the point, McKendrick." She leans back in her seat with a contented sigh. "No cameras, no microphones, no Daphne asking us about our 'relationship journey.' Just trees, mountains, and blessed silence."

The truck bounces over a particularly nasty rut, and Jo grabs the dash to steady herself. I can't help but grin at her momentary look of alarm.

"Careful there, Rodeo Queen. I thought you mountain folk were used to rough terrain."

"I'm used to it on horseback, not in your ancient truck that apparently has no suspension whatsoever." She spears me with a dirty look. "Seriously, when was the last time you had this thing serviced?"

"Don't insult Betsy. She's sensitive."

"You named your truck Betsy?" Jo tries to look annoyed but only manages to half stifle her smile. "How original, Clay."

"Hey, she's gotten me through years of rodeos and ranch work. Show some respect."

"Betsy hasn't earned my respect yet," Jo fires back, then grabs the overhead handle as we hit another bump. "At this rate, we'll both need back surgery before we reach the cabin."

I ease off the gas pedal, trying to navigate the worst of the ruts. The forest thickens around us, and the sunlight filters through the pine branches in dappled patterns that splash across the windshield. It's peaceful out here, the kind of quiet that makes you realize how much noise you've been living with.

"So, three days of just us," I remind her, trying to sound casual. "Any big plans, or are we winging it all the way?"

Jo stays quiet for a moment as she stares out the side window. "I was thinking about our plan—doing absolutely nothing for at least twenty-four hours. No schedule, no makeup, no pretending to be something I'm not."

"Sounds perfect." I steal a glance at her profile. The tension she's been carrying for weeks is already starting to ease, as evidenced by her shoulders. They aren't bunched up anymore. "Though I have to ask—when you say 'pretending to be something you're not,' what exactly have you been pretending to be?"

"Happy," she says without hesitation, then catches herself. "I mean, not that I'm miserable or anything. It's just..." She trails off, fidgeting with the rolled-down window. "This whole engagement thing is exhausting. Smiling on cue, going overboard with acting like we're madly in love, pretending that having cameras follow us around is totally normal."

"Yeah, well, you're not the only one feeling the strain." I navigate around a fallen branch, and Betsy's engine grumbles in protest. "Yesterday I caught myself checking my reflection in store windows, wondering if I looked 'engaged' enough."

Jo snorts. "What exactly does 'engaged enough' look like?" She makes air quotes with her fingers. "Are you supposed to have a certain glow or something?"

"According to Miranda, yes. Remember that coaching session she gave us? 'Clay, darling, you need to look at Jo like she's the only woman on earth.' As if I need instructions on how to look at you."

Jo's cheeks color slightly, and she turns back to the window. "At least you didn't have your mother shoving bridal magazines into your suitcase. I already have a dress, but Mom wants me to pick out ten outfits for before and after the nuptials. Oh, and don't get me started on the honeymoon options she came up with."

"My mom's the same way. She's already planning where to hang our wedding photos at the ranch house so they'll be ready when we get back from the honeymoon."

The truck hits another particularly vicious rut, and Jo's body jolts upward before crashing back into the seat.

"Jesus, Clay! Are you finding these holes on purpose?"

"Nope, just lucky, I guess." I glance at Jo, who's scowling. "Didn't you do up your seatbelt, darlin'?"

Her scowl deepens. "Of course I did. But I think Betsy is trying to kill me, like the car in that Stephen King movie."

"Betsy loves you, Jo, trust me." I grip the steering wheel tighter, trying to avoid the worst of the damage to what's left of this so-called road. "Look, there's the cabin."

Through a break in the trees, a small log structure comes into view, nestled against a backdrop of towering pines and jagged mountain peaks. It's rustic in the best possible way—the kind of place that promises wood-burning fireplaces and absolutely zero Wi-Fi.

"Thank goodness," Jo breathes, and I'm not sure if she's referring to our arrival or the end of Betsy's assault on her spine.

I pull up next to the cabin and kill the engine. The abrupt silence is almost overwhelming after weeks of constant noise and chatter. No cameras clicking, no producers shouting directions, no crowds cheering. Just the whisper of wind through pine needles and the distant call of a hawk.

"This is exactly what we needed, baby." I exhale a long breath I didn't know I was holding. "Listen to that."

Jo tilts her head, her hair falling in a cascade over one shoulder. "Listen to what?"

"Exactly." I grin at her. "Nothing. Just the sounds of wildlife and the wind."

We sit here for a moment, soaking in the silence. Jo's eyes close briefly, and I watch the tension visibly drain from her face. Her entire body slackens too. When she opens her eyes again, I note a softness there that I haven't seen in months.

"Come on," she finally says, unbuckling her seatbelt. "Let's check out our home for the next three days."

The cabin is everything the photos promised—rustic charm with just enough modern amenities to keep us from feeling like we've completely abandoned civilization. The main room features a stone fireplace, worn leather furniture that's seen better days but looks plenty comfortable, and large windows that frame the spectacular mountain view. The kitchen is small but functional, with a propane stove and a refrigerator that hums softly in the corner.

"Not bad," I say, dropping our bags by the door. "Your cousin has good taste."

Jo runs her hand along the rough-hewn dining table, her fingers tracing the knots in the wood. "He barely uses it anymore. Too busy with his law practice in Billings." She looks up at me with a hint of mischief. "His loss is our gain."

I wander to the back of the cabin where a narrow hallway leads to what I assume is the bedroom. One bed. Queen-size with a patchwork quilt and a horde of puffy pillows. For what I have in mind, all those pillows will come in handy.

"Clay!" Jo calls out. "You've got to see the open kitchen. It's the most beautiful thing I've ever seen."

I march over to the bar, sweep Jo up in my arms, and head straight to the bedroom. She keeps her arms around my neck until I toss her onto the plush bed. "We can admire the kitchen later. Now, it's time to get naked and do dirty things to each other."

Jo bounces on the bed and laughs, a rich, genuine sound I haven't heard in weeks. "So subtle, McKendrick. What happened to the romance?"

I lean against the doorframe, drinking in the sight of her sprawled across the quilt—and imagining her naked. "Romance? You want candlelight and rose petals? I thought we were here to be ourselves, no pretending."

She props herself up on her elbows. "And the real Clay McKendrick just tosses women onto beds and expects them to strip?"

"Only the ones who've been driving me crazy for months." I push away from the doorframe and saunter toward her. "Only the women who look at me like you're looking at me right now."

"And how exactly am I looking at you?" Her voice has dropped to that husky tone that makes my pulse quicken.

"Like you're imagining me fucking you."

Jo slithers across the bed, sliding off it to set her feet on the floor. "What should we do about that, honey?"

I take hold of her blouse and rip it open, buttons ticking on the floorboards. "I formulated a plan before we got in the truck this morning." I shove my hand inside her jeans, feeling the slick heat of her folds that swiftly coat my hand. "Step one, tear your clothes off. Step two, get on your knees in front of me. Step three, follow all subsequent commands until I give you permission to stop. Understand?"

"Yes, Clay." She reaches down as if to stroke her wet flesh.

I seize her wrist. "Uh-uh-uh, Jo. I'm in command now."

Chapter Twenty-Four
Down & Dirty

Jo's breaths shorten, her chest heaving, while a delicate sprinkling of pink dusts her cheeks. The scent of her hunger for me permeates the air, and every time she wriggles her hips, it makes her tits wriggle too. Jo and I have done plenty of dirty things together, but nothing like what I dreamed up a minute ago. I need to take her hard, make her scream—all while I remain in control of her desire until I allow her to come.

She's already naked. And my dick is already swollen.

"You're going to be a good girl for me, aren't you, Jo?" My voice has grown rougher with need as I reach for the silk scarf draped over the chair. I'd bought it last week while Jo was in the grocery store. Now, her eyes widen, the pupils dilating as she watches me test the fabric between my hands.

"Clay…" she exhales, but there's no protest in her voice. Only anticipation.

I move closer, the scarf trailing along her collarbone. "I asked you a question."

"Yes." The word comes out barely above a whisper. "Yes, I'll be good."

I circle behind her, gathering her wrists gently. "Obedient girls get rewarded."

Her pulse hammers against my fingertips as I bind her hands behind her back, not tight enough to hurt but secure enough that she can't touch me—or herself. And that's exactly what I want.

"I'll do anything you want," she whispers, a tremble in her voice that makes my cock throb. "I'll do anything for you, anything at all. The dirtier the better."

"That's what I like to hear, baby."

I tug the silk knot once more, testing its hold before trailing my fingers up her spine. Every vertebra gets a touch, a reminder that I'm mapping every inch of her. Her breath hitches when I reach her nape, tangling my fingers in her auburn hair. With a gentle but firm grip, I tilt her head back until her eyes meet mine.

"If this gets too intense for you, baby, just tell me so."

Jo nods, her throat working as she swallows. "Will you let me go down on you?"

"Not just yet. I've got plans for you." I graze my lips over one nipple, making her shiver. "Now, get on your knees."

She hesitates for half a heartbeat—not in resistance, but in that delicious space between anticipation and surrender. I watch her eyes, darkened with desire, as she slowly lowers herself to her knees before me. The movement is graceful despite her bound hands, and the vulnerability in her posture sends a surge of possessive heat through my veins.

"That's it," I growl, my hand still tangled in her hair. "Look at me, Jo."

She tilts her face up, and the sight nearly undoes me—her lips parted, cheeks flushed, those green eyes blazing with a mix of defiance and surrender that's uniquely hers. Even on her knees, there's something untamed about Jo Callahan that makes conquering her all the sweeter.

I trace my thumb across her bottom lip, feeling her quick breath against my skin. "You know what I want to do to you?"

She shakes her head. "Don't care. Whatever you want, I want too."

My cock has grown so hard that I have no choice now. I strip off my clothes, facing away from her. When I glance over my shoulder, she's gnawing on her lip, desperation clear in her expression. Then I turn around, holding my stiff cock with one hand. Jo whimpers. Her attention is focused on my swollen dick and the redness at its tip. She pants even harder as if my cock is the only sustenance she wants.

I move just near enough that when I brush my cock over her chest, a small drop of liquid glistens there. "You want a taste, baby?"

Jo nods frantically, her tongue darting out to wet her lips.

I come closer, trailing my cock across her collarbone, leaving a glistening path on her skin. When I brush the head against her parted lips, she strains forward, eager to take me in her mouth, but I pull back just enough to deny her.

"Not yet, darlin'." I cup her jaw, my thumb pressing gently against her cheek. "I want to hear you beg for it."

A flash of that trademark Callahan stubbornness crosses her features before melting back into raw need. With her hands bound behind her back, she can't reach for me—can't control anything. The realization makes her pupils dilate even further.

"Please," she whispers, her voice shaky. "I need to taste you, Clay. Please let me."

I trace my cock along her lips again, letting her feel how hard I am for her. "Tell me exactly what you want to do."

"I want to suck your dick until you can't think straight." Her voice is husky with lust. "I want to feel you hit the back of my throat while you explode in my mouth. Please, Clay, please."

The desperation in her voice is my undoing. I guide myself to her eager mouth, watching as her lips close around me. The wet heat of her tongue sends a jolt of pleasure up my spine.

"That's it," I groan, threading my fingers through her hair. "Take all of me."

With her hands bound, Jo can't control the pace or depth. She's completely at my mercy as I guide her head, setting a rhythm that has her moaning around my length. The vibration nearly buckles my knees. I know I'll come any second, but I don't want that just yet. I hoist Jo off the floor, tossing her onto the bed. A small squeak escapes her lips. She lies there, legs splayed, one arm above her head while the other rests on her thigh.

Fuck, I can't wait any longer.

I untie the scarf and pounce on her. "Spread your legs, Jo. Now."

The moment she does that, I clasp her hands above her head and start pounding into her with a ferocity that makes the headboard slam against the wall. Jo cries out, her back arching off the mattress as I drive into her slick heat. The sensation is overwhelming—she's so wet, so tight around me that I have to grit my teeth to maintain control. The scent of her cream fills the air.

"Clay!" she exclaims, her legs wrapping around my waist, pulling me deeper. "Oh God, yes!"

I keep her wrists pinned with one hand while the other grips her hip, angling her just right so I can hit that spot inside her that makes her eyes roll back. Her breasts bounce with every thrust, and I can't resist dipping my head to capture one nipple between my teeth, tugging just enough to make her whimper.

"You like that?" I growl against her skin, releasing her hands to grip both her hips now. "You like being fucked this way, don't you?"

"Yes, oh yes, I need to come, Clay, please."

Though I can't speak, and my heart pounds like a bass drum, I grunt and nod to show her I understand. It's time to make us both come. I push my hand between our bodies, finding her swollen clit with my thumb. The moment I touch her there, she jerks and cries out as if she's been struck by lightning.

"Not yet," I command, even as my own control frays at the edges. "Wait for me, baby."

Jo's head thrashes against the pillow, her nails digging into my shoulders. "I can't—Clay, I can't hold back—"

"Yes, you can." I slow my thrusts to deep, deliberate strokes that have her sobbing with need. "You're going to wait until I tell you. Show me how good you can be."

The effort it takes her to obey is written across her face—the way her teeth sink into her bottom lip, how her whole body trembles with the strain of holding back her release. It's the most beautiful fucking thing I've ever seen.

My rhythm becomes erratic as I feel my own release building, coiling tight at the base of my spine. Jo's internal muscles clench around me, and I know she's fighting a losing battle.

"Please," she begs, her voice breaking. "Clay, I need to—"

"Now," I snarl, pressing hard circles against her clit. "Come for me now, Jo."

The permission breaks something loose inside her. She shatters beneath me with a cry that might wake the wildlife, her body arching like a bow as waves of pleasure crash through her. The sight of her coming undone triggers my own release, and I drive into her one final time, burying myself to the hilt as I empty myself inside her with a hoarse shout.

"Jolene!"

For several moments, there's nothing but our ragged breathing and the thundering of our hearts. Then I finally collapse beside her, pulling her sweat-slicked body against me.

"Holy shit," Jo gasps, her body still quivering with aftershocks. Her hair is a wild tangle splayed across the pillow, her skin flushed and glistening. "That was...I don't even have words...It was never like this before."

I press my lips to her temple, tasting salt and sweetness there. "You okay, Jo?"

"Better than okay." She turns her face toward mine, her pupils dilated from sheer satisfaction. "I didn't know you had that in you, McKendrick."

A lazy smile tugs at my mouth. "There's a lot you still don't know about me yet."

Jo's fingertips trace the line of my jaw, her touch feather-light. "I think I like discovering your secrets."

I catch her hand, pressing a kiss to her palm. Something protective and possessive surges through me as I take in the sight of her—completely undone, completely mine. We aren't quite married yet, but already I know we will never split up, not even after a thousand years.

Our connection is epic and forever.

Chapter Twenty-Five
The Season Ends

October has become our time for endings. Not only has the reality show completed its first season, but Jo and I will be ending our engagement. We haven't split up. Instead, we're rushing headlong into the best kind of ending, the sort that morphs into a happily ever after when we finally tie the knot. As for the reality series… Miranda wanted us to stay for another season—or hopefully forever—but we politely declined the offer. It's time we got back to normal life.

I'm not sure what normal life means for us anymore. The cameras have been gone for two weeks, and I keep catching myself looking over my shoulder, expecting to see Miranda lurking in a corner with her clipboard.

Jo's different now—more relaxed, but also restless. She's been spending extra hours at the barn, working with Blaze and trying out some new ideas for the women's roping team. The rodeo season winds down in three weeks, and Jo is sitting pretty in second place for the WPRA standings. Close enough to taste that championship and make her crazy with wanting it. Thunder and I have gotten back on the circuit too, even winning a few more titles. But we plan on scaling back our rodeo activities somewhat.

Why? Because it's time to get married. I plan on popping the question tonight, after Jo's last rodeo event of the season.

Not that she knows about that. As far as Jo's concerned, we're heading to the Silver Spurs Arena for just another qualifier. She's been so focused on training that she hasn't noticed me sneaking around with Casey, her father, and her brother while finalizing the details. My mom and Sarah have gotten involved too. Jo also hasn't noticed the way my mother keeps calling with random questions about Jo's favorite flowers and cake flavors.

I watch while Jo tightens Blaze's cinch one last time. Her movements are precise, practiced, methodical, deliberate. It's the same way she approaches our relationship ever since the Hollywood types had gone home. Like she's savoring every moment now that it belongs to just us again.

Jo has her face buried in a rodeo magazine and doesn't glance up even when she smiles. "You're staring again, Clay."

"Can't help it. My fiancée's too damn gorgeous not to gawk at."

Jo turns toward me, finally looking my way. "We won't be engaged for much longer. Pretty soon, we'll have to train ourselves to call each other husband and wife."

"Think you can handle that?"

Her crooked smile, the one that first caught my eye more than a year ago, makes my pulse jump. "Might take some practice. Mrs. McKendrick has a nice ring to it though."

Mrs. McKendrick. Damn, I like the sound of that more than I thought I would. The ring box is in my truck, and I struggle against the urge to check on it for the tenth time today. Can't wait to slip that gold band onto her finger—and keep it there for a lifetime.

"You nervous about tonight?" I ask, nodding toward Blaze.

Jo's expression has shifted into that familiar intensity she always has before an event. "Second place isn't good enough. Not when I'm this close." She runs her hand along Blaze's neck, and the mare nuzzles her. "We've worked too hard to settle for second."

"You'll get it." The certainty in my voice surprises even me, but it's true. I've watched Jo drive herself harder than she would push any horse. There's no way that championship isn't coming home with her tonight.

"You sound pretty confident," Jo says, finally looking up from Blaze to meet my eyes.

"I'm absolutely positive you'll win. I've seen what you and Blaze can do." I step closer, resting my hand on the small of her back. "Besides, I've got a good feeling about tonight."

Jo narrows her eyes, studying my face. "You're acting weird lately."

"Am I?" My heart's hammering so hard I'm surprised she can't hear it.

"Yeah. Like you're hiding something." She pokes my chest with one finger. "Tell me what's going on, McKendrick."

I catch her hand and bring it to my lips, pressing a kiss against her callused palm. "Hey, have you heard anything about Brock and Maddie?"

Evasion is always a winning strategy when you're trying to hide a secret from your fiancée. A good secret.

Jo narrows her gaze even more, clearly aware that I'm dodging her question, but the mention of Brock Sterling's name does exactly what I hoped it would. It distracts her completely. "Maddie texted me yesterday. Apparently, Brock's been pestering her for another date since that charity auction." Jo shakes her head, turning back to adjust Blaze's bridle. "I told her to run for the hills. Once a snake, always a snake."

"Can't argue with that." I lean against the stall door, watching Jo work. The way her fingers move with such confidence, how she communicates with that horse without saying a word—it's like watching a dance they've perfected for years. "Do you believe Maddie's story? That Brock threatened to splash nude pictures of her across all the social media sites if she didn't spook her horse on purpose?"

"I don't have a single doubt," Jo confirms. "I've gotten to know Maddie over the past year, and I've learned she doesn't lie about that kind of thing. Besides, I've seen how he operates. Remember what he tried to pull with us during filming?"

I nod, remembering how Brock had cornered Jo in the barn that day, trying to convince her that I was only with her for the publicity. The cameras caught it all—his smooth talking, Jo's furious rejection, and my timely arrival that prevented things from getting uglier.

"Miranda cut that whole scene," Jo adds, shaking her head. "Said it didn't fit the 'narrative arc' they were building."

"Probably for the best. I'd have looked like a jealous hothead on national television."

Jo smirks. "You are a jealous hothead."

"Only when it comes to you." I shove my hands into my jeans pockets, blowing out a heavy breath. "Well, at least Brock got what he deserved—banned from rodeo for life. Maddie only got a two-year suspension."

Jo shakes her head. "Feels like she got the raw end of that deal." She checks Blaze's legs one more time. "Maddie was defending herself, and Brock was the one who—"

"Started it all," I finish for her. "I know. But the PRCA had to make an example of them both. At least her suspension's relatively short."

Jo makes a noncommittal sound, but I can tell she's still bothered by the situation. That's my woman—fiercely protective of those she cares about. It's one of the thousand reasons I love her.

"We should head out." I check my watch. "Don't want to be late for the big event."

"You mean my qualifier?" Jo raises her eyebrows. "Since when are you Mr. Punctuality?"

I shrug, trying to keep my expression neutral. "Just eager to see you kick some ass out there. Plus, I promised your dad we'd meet him early."

Jo gives me a look that says she's not entirely buying it, but she finishes with Blaze's tack and leads the mare out of the stall. "Fine, but you're acting jumpy as a long-tailed cat in a room full of rocking chairs."

"Ha-ha." I swat her ass. "Get out there, Jolene, and whup all the other girls.

She grasps my ass, giving it a squeeze. "After that, I'll get to watch you riding the baddest bull in rodeo. You know how that always makes me horny."

The drive to Silver Spurs Arena takes forty minutes, and Jo spends most of it going over her strategy, talking through the cloverleaf pattern for what must be the hundredth time this week. I nod and make the right noises at the right moments, but my mind keeps drifting back to the blue velvet box tucked safely in my jacket pocket. I'd moved it from the dashboard when Jo wasn't looking.

When we pull into the arena parking lot, I can already see the crowd gathering. More people than usual for a qualifier, which means word's gotten out about Jo's championship run. The local news van parked near the entrance confirms it.

I nod toward the van. "Looks like you've got some media attention, darlin'."

Jo groans. "Great. Just what I need—extra pressure." She hops out of the truck and starts unloading Blaze. "I hate when the media shows up. Makes everything feel so…commercial."

"Of course reporters are here. It's official, baby. You're about to make history."

She pauses, her hand on Blaze's lead rope. "Don't jinx it."

"No such thing as jinxing anything." I grab her gear bag and sling it over my shoulder. "Besides, after all that reality TV nonsense, a local news crew shouldn't bother you one bit."

Jo rolls her eyes, but I can see the tension in her shoulders easing a little. "At least these reporters won't ask me to cry on cue or manufacture drama with my fiancé."

"That's the spirit." I rest my hand on the small of her back as we lead Blaze toward the competitors' area. "Just another day at the office."

Jo's father spots us before we see him, his deep voice carrying over the pre-rodeo bustle.

"Jo! Clay! Over here!" Hank Callahan waves his cowboy hat above the crowd, and I spot Jo's brother Levi standing next to him, both of them grinning like they've won the lottery.

"Dad's awfully excited for a qualifier," Jo mutters under her breath, but she's smiling as we make our way over to them.

Hank pulls Jo into a bear hug that lifts her clean off the ground. "There's my champion daughter!"

"Dad, I haven't won anything yet," Jo protests, but she's laughing.

"Baloney," Hank waves her off, then claps me on the shoulder hard enough to rattle my teeth. "Clay, good to see you, son."

Levi steps forward, and there's something in his expression that tells me he knows. Both our families know what's coming tonight, but keeping this secret is apparently harder for the Callahan men than I thought it would be.

"Big night," Levi says, trying to sound casual but failing miserably. "Really big night."

Jo narrows her eyes, glancing between her father and brother. "Okay, what's going on? You're both acting so weird that I'm about ready to call a psychiatrist."

"Nothing's going on," Hank says quickly. "Can't a father be excited about his daughter competing in a rodeo?"

"Since when do you get this worked up about a qualifier?" Jo crosses her arms. "And why are you both grinning like idiots?"

I jump in before one of them cracks under pressure. "Maybe they're just proud of you. You're about to clinch the championship, Jo."

She studies all three of us with those sharp green eyes, and I can practically see the wheels turning in her head. Jo's always been too smart for her own good.

"I need to get Blaze settled," she finally tells us, though suspicion still lingers in her voice. "You three can stand around acting mysterious all you want, but I've got work to do."

She leads Blaze toward the competitor stalls, leaving the three of us standing here like guilty schoolboys.

Once Jo is out of earshot, I squint hard at Hank and Levi. "Smooth, guys, real smooth."

"Sorry," Levi grins sheepishly. "I'm terrible at keeping secrets from Jo. Always have been."

Hank chuckles. "Remember when we tried to surprise her for her sixteenth birthday? She figured it out three days early."

"Well, let's try not to spill the beans for at least another few hours," I suggest, checking my watch again. "The surprise won't work if she knows it's coming."

"Speaking of which…" Hank's expression grows serious. "Have you got everything you need? The ring, the flowers, all that?"

I pat my jacket pocket reflexively. "Ring's right here. Your wife handled the flowers, and Casey took care of the photographer." My throat feels tight suddenly. "Think she'll say yes?"

Levi snorts. "Are you kidding me? Jo's been planning your wedding since the cameras stopped rolling. She's got three different venues picked out and a whole Pinterest board dedicated to cowboy wedding themes."

"She's got a Pinterest board?" That's news to me.

"Oh-ho yeah," Hank says. "Caught her looking at wedding dresses on her laptop last week. When I asked about it, she turned red as a tomato and slammed the thing shut."

Relief floods through me, loosening the knot in my chest. "Good to know I'm not the only one thinking about making this official."

"Son, that girl's been crazy about you since day one," Hank assures me, clapping my shoulder again. "Even when she was swearing up and down that she'd never date another cowboy."

I chuckle, remembering how stubborn Jo had been when we first met. "She's still the most hardheaded woman I've ever known."

"Callahan family trait," Levi confirms with a wink. "Now go help her with Blaze before she gets suspicious."

I find Jo in the stall area, methodically brushing Blaze's gleaming coat. Her pre-competition ritual hasn't changed since I've known her—brush, check tack, walk the pattern in her mind, then sit quietly with her horse for ten minutes before heading to the gate.

"Need any help?" I ask, leaning against the stall door.

Jo doesn't look up, but her lips curve into a small smile.

I open my mouth to speak but don't get the chance. Buck Hawkins jogs up to me.

"Kid, we've got something special for you. Your dad came up with the idea."

"What are you old farts up to now?"

"You'll see."

Chapter Twenty-Six
The Big Race

Buck shoves two fingers in his mouth, letting out an ear-piercing whistle to summon…my dad. "Come on, Jeb, pick up the pace!"

Dad is out of breath by the time he reaches us, but he still manages to boss us around. "Come on, Clay. We've got a big surprise for you and Jo."

"What is it?"

My father looks too smug, which makes me worry about what these old farts have cooked up. "Should we tell him now, Buck?"

"Sure, why not."

Dad smirks even more. "It's a race to find out who's the fastest on a horse—you or Jo."

I groan. "A race? Now? Jo's about to compete for the championship."

Buck slaps me on the back. "Exactly why it's perfect timing, kid. Nothing like a little friendly competition between future spouses to get the blood pumping before a big event."

Jo finally glances up from Blaze, hesitating mid-stroke as she brushes her horse. Jo has a canny glint in her eyes that I know so well. "Did someone mention a race?"

"Don't even think about it," I warn her. "You need to focus on your run."

"I am focused," Jo counters, stepping out of the stall. "And beating you in a race might be just what I need to loosen up."

Dad's grinning like he just won the lottery. "That's the spirit, Jo! We've set up a simple course—just around the arena once and back. Nothing that will interfere with your championship run."

I lift my brows. "Don't mind losing to a superior rider then, hey?"

She tilts her up in that stubborn way that means she's fallen into my trap. "If you think you'll win against me, you are sorely mistaken, McKendrick."

"Thunder is bigger than Blaze. You might get hurt because these two troublemakers think a race is a good idea." I glare at Dad and Buck. "What if something happens? What if she falls?"

"Clay." Jo's voice takes on a softer tone, and she steps closer to lay her hand on my chest. "I've been riding longer than I've been walking, and I race every single time I perform at a rodeo. It's called barrel *racing* for a reason. And a simple lap around the arena isn't going to hurt anything."

The ring box feels like it's burning a hole through my pocket. But I suddenly realize she's right. We're both experienced riders, and I'm being overprotective. "Okay, Jo. Let's do it."

"Thunder's already saddled," Dad informs me, jerking his thumb toward where my horse waits. "Figured you'd see reason eventually."

"You had this planned from the start, for sure." I'm already walking toward Thunder, my competitive streak overriding my common sense. If Jo wants a race, she'll get one—and I'll make damn sure she doesn't win easily enough to get cocky before her championship run.

Jo is already leading Blaze toward the arena, her movements fluid and confident as always. My fiancée is a force of nature. The mare prances a bit—sensing the competitive energy between me and Jo, no doubt. Other competitors and their families are starting to fill the stands as the word spreads faster. Jolene Callahan and Clay McKendrick are about to square off.

I swing up into Thunder's saddle. It's been too long since Jo and I went head-to-head on horseback.

Buck positions himself at the starting line, raising his hat like some kind of makeshift flag. "Once around the arena—that's it. Nothing fancy, nothing dangerous. First one back to this spot wins."

Jo settles into her saddle with her usual easy grace and winks at me. "Hope you're ready to eat my dust, McKendrick."

"In your dreams, Callahan."

We line up side by side, and I can feel the familiar electricity crackling between us. This is how it's always been with Jo—everything turns into a competition, and neither of us knows how to back down.

Buck is clearly reveling in his role as the guy who starts the race. "On your mark! Get set!" Buck pauses, drawing out the moment until Jo and I both lean forward in our saddles. "GO!"

We explode from the starting line amid the thundering hooves and flying dirt. Jo and Blaze take an early lead, the mare's powerful hindquarters propelling them forward with graceful precision. Thunder responds to my subtle leg cues, stretching his neck as we surge after the girls. The arena is large enough to let our horses hit their stride in no time. Jo glances over her shoulder, that competitive fire sparking in her eyes as she sees me gaining on her. She leans over Blaze's neck, whispering something I can't hear that makes the mare kick into gear.

"Come on, boy," I urge Thunder, feeling his muscles bunch beneath me as we round the first turn. The big guy has always been good on the corners, and he doesn't disappoint now, cutting the angle just enough to put us neck and neck with Jo and Blaze.

"Thought you'd be faster than that!" I shout, grinning as we blast down the straightaway.

Jo doesn't waste any breath responding. She flashes me a cocky grin, and I respond in kind. She's beautiful like this—her hair streaming behind her, every one of her muscles moving in perfect harmony with Blaze. We're shoulder to shoulder as we approach the final turn, close enough that I can hear Jo's rhythmic breathing and see the freckles that stand out against her creamy skin. The crowd along the fence is cheering. Jo's eyes narrow in concentration as her legs grip Blaze's sides with confident precision.

The final turn looms ahead, and I know this is where the race will be decided. Thunder shifts beneath me, his muscles tensing and flexing as we prepare to make our move. Jo gets ready too, with a subtle adjustment of her position and the way she shortens her reins a fraction.

"Let's show them what we've got," I tell Thunder, and he responds instantly.

We take the turn wide, giving Jo the inside track, but Thunder's powerful stride eats up the ground as we straighten for the final stretch. The cheers of the crowd escalate into a dull roar in my ears as we pull even with Blaze, then inch ahead.

Surprise flashes over Jo's face before hardening into pure determination. She clicks to Blaze, and the mare digs deep, finding that reserve of energy that has won her so many championships. We're in perfect sync, stride for stride, as we barrel toward the finish line where Buck stands waving his hat wildly.

"Come on, Clay, kick her ass!" I hear my dad hollering somewhere in the crowd, and when I take a quick glance, I see my whole family cheering.

The finish line rushes toward us. Neither horse gives an inch. I can feel Thunder's heart hammering beneath me, matching my own. Jo's eyes meet mine for a split second—fierce, focused, and alive with joy. This is us at our core, two competitors who push each other to our best and beyond. We flash past Buck in a cloud of dust, so close that even he can't tell who crossed the finish line first. Thunder and Blaze gradually slow down until they finally halt.

"It's a tie!" Buck announces, throwing his hat in the air. "Photo finish! Never seen anything like it in all my years!"

The crowd erupts in cheers and good-natured arguments about who actually won. Jo and I circle back toward each other, both our horses still prancing with leftover adrenaline.

"Not bad for a nobody from the middle of nowhere," Jo teases, her cheeks flushed and eyes sparkling. She's breathing hard, and there's a piece of hay stuck in her hair that makes me want to reach over and pluck it out.

"Nobody? I'm a TV star, remember?"

"We both were, Clay, in case you forgot. But at least I know how to tenderize a steak properly." She grins, patting Blaze's neck. "Good thing it was a tie, or I might've had to gloat."

"You would've lost that bet." I lean forward in my saddle. "But I've got a consolation prize for you."

Her brows furrow. Confused Jo is the cutest version of her.

I bring Thunder up alongside Blaze, then reach over to pull Jo onto my lap. The arena goes silent—until I pull out the ring box.

Jo's eyes bulge, and her lips fall open in shock as she gapes at the small velvet box. Her weight is warm across my lap, solid and real, and suddenly my heart is galloping faster than Thunder ever could.

"Clay McKendrick, what are you doing?" she whispers, just loud enough for me to hear.

The crowd around us has gone completely silent. I can feel a passel of eyes on us, but all I can see is Jo—the freckles that sprinkle her nose and cheeks, the slight tremble in her hands as she grips Thunder's mane for balance. "I'm improvising, Jo."

This wasn't how I planned it, but it'll work. The box feels slick in my sweaty palm. "I was going to wait until after your championship run, but—"

"But you're too stubborn and impatient," she finishes, an affectionate smile tugging at the corners of her mouth. But her eyes are suspiciously bright, and I can feel the smallest tremor running through her body where she's pressed against me.

"Maybe I am impatient," I admit, balancing her carefully on Thunder's back as I flip open the box with my thumb. The simple diamond catches the afternoon sunlight, sending prisms dancing across Jo's face. "But I've also been waiting my whole life for this moment."

Jo's lips fall open, and she swallows hard. "Clay..."

"I had a whole speech planned. About how we've been circling each other since we first met in Tampa. About how no one pushes me or challenges me or understands me like you do."

The crowd has gone silent. Buck, my dad, the championship—none of it matters now. It's just Jo and me, suspended in this moment on Thunder's back.

"But the truth is simple, Jo. I love you. I love how you never let me win anything easily. I love how you talk to your horse like she's your best friend. I love that you put hot sauce on everything, even ice cream that one time."

She laughs through what might be tears. "That was a dare from your sister."

"I love that you accepted the dare." I shift her slightly, making sure she's secure. "I love your stubborn streak and your competitive fire and the way you hum when you're concentrating. I love that you're brave enough to chase championships and foolish enough to race me five minutes before the biggest ride of your season."

"Clay..." Her voice breaks slightly as her eyes turn glossy with tears she's trying to stave off.

"Jolene Luella Callahan, will you marry me? Will you become my wife, my partner, the one person who really knows me and always tells me the God's honest truth. Please, say yes so I can spend the rest of my life trying to keep up with you."

Jo started crying a minute ago, but now the tears are streaming down her cheeks. "Yes, Clay, yes! Of course I'll marry you." She flings her arms around my neck, nearly unseating us both from Thunder's back. "Yes, I'll marry you, Clay McKendrick. Yes to everything you just said."

The crowd goes insane. Buck's whooping carries over everyone else's cheers, and I'm pretty sure I hear my dad yelling something about it being about damn time. But I'm too busy kissing Jo to care about anything else.

Chapter Twenty-Seven
Cowboy Wedding

Three and a half weeks after the big race between me and Jo, we leave the rodeo world behind—for the moment. Our wedding takes precedence over everything else, and I can't wait to finally see the dress Jo picked out. My sister Sarah has seen it. So has Jo's sister Casey. It's top secret for the rest of us, and breaching the veil of secrecy imposes a death sentence.

Okay, nobody will actually die.

I couldn't resist a little hyperbole, that's all.

But Jo is serious about keeping her dress under wraps. She actually made Sarah sign what she called a "non-disclosure agreement," which was really just a napkin from the diner where they were eating during their wedding discussions.

Sarah took it seriously anyway. My sister's always been a sucker for dramatic gestures.

"You'll see it when everyone else sees it," Jo tells me for the hundredth time when I try to wheedle information out of her. She's got that stubborn set to her jaw that means I'm not getting anywhere, no matter how much I crank up the charm.

"Come on, darlin'. How about a hint? A tiny one?" I'm trailing after her as she marches through the bridal shop like a woman on a mission. "Is it white? Please tell me it's at least white."

Jo stops so abruptly that I nearly crash into her. When she turns around, I detect the telltale signs of mischief brewing in those beautiful green eyes of hers. But Jo's been dropping hints like breadcrumbs, and I've been following every single one. Yesterday she mentioned something about "layers that move like water," which sounds either ridiculously romantic or like she's planning to wear a fishing net.

Knowing Jo, it could go either way.

We're holed up in the bridal suite at the Cheyenne Grand—a fancy name for what amounts to a glorified hotel room with extra mirrors and a champagne bucket that's been empty since we arrived. Jo has been locked in the adjoining room with my sister while I pace around like a caged bull. I adjust my tie for the hundredth time since I have nothing else to do right now.

"Quit fidgeting," Sarah says from the other side of the bathroom door. Behind that slab of wood, she's issuing orders to my fiancée. "You look beautiful, Jo."

"I look like I'm about to throw up," my wife-to-be snarls.

"Yeah, Clay looks that way too."

Casey clucks her tongue. "That's the groom look. It's traditional."

Yes, my sister is helping Jo's sister get my fiancée ready for that walk down the aisle. I catch my reflection in one of the mirrors in the living room, and I have to admit Casey's right. My face has gone pale—which I know because I saw my reflection in the window—and there's a wild look in my eyes that suggests I might bolt at any second. Which is ridiculous, because I've never wanted anything more than I want to marry Jo Callahan.

"Five minutes!" Sarah shouts, and my stomach drops to somewhere around my boots.

I hear Jo muttering something that sounds suspiciously like a string of curse words that would make a sailor blush. Then I hear Casey's voice, gentle but firm: "Breathe, Jo. In through your nose, out through your mouth. Just like you do before a run."

"This is nothing like that," Jo snaps back. "Before a run, I'm in control. I know what my horse is going to do, I know the pattern, I know the course. This is—this is—"

"You're marrying the man you love, your soulmate," Casey finishes softly. "The same man who challenged you to that race three weeks ago and who's been pacing a hole in the carpet in front of that door for the past hour."

"I can hear him," Jo mutters, and I freeze mid-step. "Clay, if you don't stop wearing out that floor, I'm going to come out there and tie you to a chair."

"Promise?" I reply, which earns me a snort of laughter from her side of the door.

"See?" Casey says. "You're already feeling better."

More rustling sounds suggest the presence of fabric, or possibly tissue paper. Yeah, right, Jo's dress is made of paper. Maybe she's wrestling with whatever contraption she plans to walk down the aisle in. Is it simple? Elaborate? Does it have those little buttons that go all the way up the back? Because if it does, I'm going to have my work cut out for me later tonight.

"Time!" Sarah announces, and the butterflies in my stomach start flapping again.

I hear the shuffle of movement beyond the door and whispered encouragements followed by silence. The kind that stretches out for what feels like forever.

"Clay?" Jo's voice comes through the wall, softer now and uncertain in a way that makes my throat go dry.

"I'm here, darlin'."

"Are you sure about this, Clay? Because once we do this thing, you're stuck with me. Grumpy mornings, competitive streak, and all my weird habits."

I press my palm against the wall, wishing I could touch her face instead of painted drywall. "Jo, I've been sure since the day you told me I couldn't rope worth a damn and then proceeded to show me how it's done."

"I was just giving you a hard time," she explains with a laugh that catches slightly at the end. I can picture her perfectly—hand pressed to her mouth, eyes glistening with the first sign of tears. "Even then, I knew you were special, not like any other cowboy."

"You amazed me from the moment I caught sight of you in the arena in Tampa, racing around those barrels like it was the simplest thing in the world."

Sweet little laugh, barely audible, whispers out of her. "Back then, I gave you no reason to like me, much less love me."

I lean my forehead against the wall. "Every second with you has been worthwhile. I wouldn't trade any of it, not for a million dollars."

Another silence follows, and I begin to wonder if she's crying. Jo doesn't cry often. She's more likely to punch something when she's emotional—but weddings have a way of bringing out unexpected reactions in people.

"Clay McKendrick," she finally says, her voice steady now, "I'm about to walk down that aisle and make you the happiest man in the West."

"You already have, darlin'. Everything else is just paperwork."

Sarah clears her throat loudly. "If you two are done having a moment through drywall, it's time to get this show on the road. Clay, get your butt downstairs to the altar before I drag you there myself."

I straighten my shoulders and take one last look in the mirror. The man staring back at me looks like he's about to either win the lottery or get trampled by a bronc—maybe both. I adjust my bolo tie one final time and head for the door. "See you down there, Mrs. McKendrick."

"I'm not your missus yet," Jo shoots back, but there's warmth in her voice now instead of panic. "But ask me again in ten minutes."

The walk down to the lobby feels like the longest ride of my life. The Cheyenne Grand has been transformed into something that looks like a cross between a western chapel and a garden party. White roses and baby's breath are wound around the rustic wooden archway where I'll be standing in approximately thirty seconds. My hands are sweating, and I resist the urge to wipe them on my pants.

The string quartet Casey insisted on hiring has begun to play a song that sounds vaguely familiar, probably because it's been stuck in my head for the past week during rehearsals. I move into my position next to Pastor Williams, an older man with a wrinkled face who's officiated more cowboy weddings than he can count. The man wears the patient expression of someone who's seen plenty of nervous grooms.

"Breathe, son," he murmurs out of the corner of his mouth. "I've yet to have one pass out on me, and I don't plan to start today."

"Yes, sir." I straighten my shoulders and gaze out at the assembled crowd. It's smaller than the usual wedding—just family and close friends, the way Jo and I both wanted it. My parents are seated in the front row with Dad looking uncomfortable in his Sunday suit but proud as a peacock. Mom dabs at her eyes with a lace handkerchief she's been carrying around all morning. Jo's folks are seated across the aisle. Hank

Callahan sits up straight, seemingly unbothered by the solemnity of the occasion. Then I see him dab at his eyes, like my mother had done, and I realize Hank's just as emotional as the rest of us.

The music shifts, and my pulse kicks into overdrive. This is it. The big moment.

Casey appears first, sashaying down the aisle looking elegant in a dusty rose dress that complements her dark hair. She catches my eye and gives me a reassuring smile before taking her place across from where I'm standing. Then Sarah follows, wearing the same bridesmaid dress as Casey. She holds her bouquet in both hands winking at me as she passes, which somehow makes me feel both better and worse at the same time.

The music swells, and it's a song I recognize now—"Canon in D," because Jo said if we were doing this wedding thing, we were going to do it right. The doors at the back of the lobby swing open, and I suddenly forget how to breathe.

Jo takes my breath away, looking so beautiful that's she reminds me of a fairy-tale princess or something out of a half-forgotten dream. The dress—God, the dress—is everything I imagined and nothing like I expected all at once. The ivory silk seems to shimmer in the natural light and moves exactly like water, just the way she hinted. It's simple but elegant, with a neckline that accentuates her lovely body and sleeves that somehow manage to be both demure and sexy as hell. Her auburn hair is swept up in some complicated arrangement that Casey probably spent an hour on, with a few loose strands framing her face.

But it's her expression that nearly brings me to my knees. The panic upstairs in the bathroom is gone, replaced by a mix of pure joy and conviction. She's looking straight at me like I'm the only person in the room. Her father walks beside her, and I can see the exact moment he transitions from protective dad to proud father giving away his daughter. When they reach the altar, he shakes my hand vigorously.

"Take care of her, son," he says quietly, and there's no threat in it—just a father's love wrapped up in four simple words.

"Yes, sir. You have my word."

I offer my arm, and Jo accepts it. The moment her fingers curl around my elbow, the world settles back into place. All the nervous energy that's been eating me alive for the past hour just... disappears.

"You look like a fairy-tale cowboy." She roves her gaze over me, admiring my pressed suit with obvious appreciation. "Almost didn't recognize you without hay in your hair."

"Jo, you…" My voice fails me completely. I clear my throat and try again. "Jo, you're the most beautiful thing I've ever seen."

Her cheeks flush pink, but she doesn't look away. "Told you it was worth the wait."

Pastor Williams clears his throat gently, and we both turn to face him, though I can't seem to stop stealing glances at Jo. The way the light catches in her hair, the slight tremor in her hands as she grips her bouquet, the freckles across her nose that she didn't bother to hide with makeup because she knows I love them.

"Dearly beloved," Pastor Williams begins, his voice carrying through the transformed hotel lobby. "We are gathered here today…"

I try to focus on his words, I really do, but Jo is standing beside me, and my brain can't seem to hold on to anything except the vision of her. I catch fragments of the pastor's speech—something about love and commitment and the joining of two souls—but all I can focus on is the woman at my side and the miracle that she's about to become my wife.

When it comes time for the vows, Jo turns to face me fully. Her green eyes are bright with unshed tears, but her voice is steady.

"I never thought I'd be here," she begins, and the raw honesty in her voice makes my throat tighten. "Standing in fancy shoes, wearing silk, promising forever to a man who once told me my roping technique needed work."

A ripple of laughter moves through the crowd, and I can't help but grin. That particular conversation had ended with her dumping a water bucket over my head.

"But here's the thing about you, Clay McKendrick—you never let me settle for good enough. You push me to be better, stronger, braver than I thought I could be. And somehow, you make me want to be soft too. You taught me to trust in something bigger than just myself."

She pauses, and I watch a single tear escape down her cheek. I want to reach out and brush it away, but I can't move an inch.

"Clay, I promise to love your stubborn streak, even when it drives me crazy. I promise to support your dreams, even the ones that scare me. And I promise to never, ever let you win a race just because we're married."

The laughter bubbles up in the crowd, and even Pastor Williams cracks a smile. Jo's grin is pure teasing now, and I shake my head at her while smiling.

"My turn?" I ask, and she nods, biting her lip in the cutest way. "Jolene Callahan, you stole my heart the first time I saw you in Tampa. Your hat was askew, your boots were muddy, and you were yelling at a judge who made a bad call. I thought, 'Now there's a woman who knows her own mind.'"

Jo's eyes sparkle with the memory, and I can see her fighting to maintain her composure.

"I didn't plan on falling in love with the most stubborn woman in three states. I didn't plan on spending half my life arguing about proper rope technique or whose turn it is to feed the horses. But darlin', I wouldn't trade a single second of it."

My voice hitches, and I take a deep breath before continuing. The entire room has gone silent, hanging on every word. "Jolene Callahan, I promise to stand beside you in the winner's circle and pick you up when you fall. I promise to respect your independence while offering my strength whenever you need it. And I promise that even on the days when we're both too stubborn to back down, I'll still choose you every single time."

I reach out and touch her cheek, brushing away a tear with my thumb. "You're my best friend, my toughest competition, and the only woman who's ever made me want to be worthy of a happy ending."

Jo's composure finally cracks, and she lets out a watery laugh that's half sob. "Damn it, Clay, you're going to make me ruin my makeup."

"Language," Pastor Williams chides gently, but his eyes are twinkling.

"Sorry, Pastor."

The ring exchange goes smoothly—thank God, because my hands are shaking so badly I'm surprised I haven't dropped the damn thing. When I slide the simple gold band onto Jo's finger, she stares down at it like she can't quite believe it's real.

"By the power vested in me by the state of Montana," Pastor Williams continues, his voice placid but his eyes sparkling, "I now pronounce you husband and wife." He hesitates, glancing between us with a knowing smile. "Clay, you may kiss your bride."

I don't need to be told twice. I slide my arm around Jo's waist, pulling her close as she rests her hands on my chest. For all her tough talk and competitiveness, the way she melts against me makes my heart fill up with a joy I've never experienced before.

"Hi, wife," I whisper.

"Hi, husband," she whispers back, and then I'm kissing her.

Time slows down as I cup Jo's face in my hands. Her eyes meet mine, but only for a moment. Then, I press my lips to hers and kiss Jo like it's the first time. I lean in, brushing my lips against hers softly at first, then with growing ardor as her arms wind around my neck. The crowd erupts in cheers and whistles, but all I can feel is Jo—the silk of her dress beneath my hands as they move to her waist, the subtle scent of wildflowers in her hair, the smile I can feel against my lips as she kisses me back with enough passion to make Pastor Williams clear his throat.

"Mrs. McKendrick," I whisper against her lips.

"That's me," she whispers back.

"Ladies and gentlemen," Pastor Williams announces, clearing his throat with the practiced timing of a man who's seen many newlyweds get carried away, "I present to you Mr. and Mrs. Clay McKendrick!"

The string quartet launches into an upbeat number as Jo and I turn to face our cheering families. We make our way back down the aisle, and I can't stop stealing glances at her profile. The happiness radiating from her is almost tangible, like heat from a summer sun. My wife. Jolene Callahan is my *wife*.

"Can we go home yet?" I whisper.

"Not yet, cowboy. We need to sign the papers first."

The next hour passes in a blur of congratulations, champagne toasts, and more hugs than I've received in the last decade combined. Jo stays glued to my side, her fingers laced through mine like she's afraid I might disappear if she lets go.

No chance of that. I found my best friend, my soul mate, the only woman who could ever make my heart race just from seeing her smile. I will never let her go. That's what a fairy-tale ending means—happy ever after.

A New Family

'm halfway through shoeing a stubborn gelding when my phone buzzes in my pocket like an angry hornet. I've been married to Jo for slightly more than a year, and I've learned that ignoring her calls is about as smart as turning your back on a bull in the chute. Pregnancy hormones have really done a number on her too. Yep, we are having a baby. But we aren't sure exactly when that will happen. Jo and I agreed we didn't want to know the gender because we'd rather be surprised.

"Hey, darlin'," I answer, wedging the phone between my shoulder and ear while I finish hammering in a nail. "Just finishing up with Thunder here and then I'll grab those jalapeño poppers you've been craving."

There's a beat of silence, then a sharp intake of breath that makes my blood run cold. "Clay." Jo's voice is tight and controlled in a way I've never heard before. "My water just broke."

The hammer slips from my hand, narrowly missing my boot. "What? But you aren't due for another week."

"Tell that to the little bronc rider in my belly who wants to kick her way out."

My pulse pounds, my ears ring, and I can't think straight. "Whuh—what should I do, Jo?"

She lets out a sharp huff. "Come into the house and call the midwife! Are all men this stupid?"

"Oh yeah, midwife." I'm already dropping Thunder's hoof and backing away from the horse stall, my hands shaking like I'm the one about to give birth. "Are you timing the contractions? Should I—"

"Clay." Jo's calm voice cuts through my panic, helping me relax a little. "Stop talking and start moving. *Now.*"

Before Jo can finish that single word, I'm running toward the house faster than I've ever moved in my life, phone still pressed to my ear. "I'm coming, darlin'. Just breathe." I see my father on the porch swing and shout to him as I keep running, "Finish shoeing Thunder for me, Dad. Jo's water broke!"

He leaps up and sprints toward the barn.

"Don't you dare tell me to breathe again, Clay McKendrick." Even in labor, my wife's got enough fire to melt steel. "I've been breathing for twenty-eight years without your help."

Of course she knows how to breathe. I'm panicking while she seems relatively calm. I burst through the kitchen door to find Jo gripping the counter, her knuckles white as fresh snow. Her auburn hair has escaped its ponytail, wild strands framing her face as she breathes through what I'm guessing is another contraction.

"Midwife," I say, fumbling for the contact list we'd stuck to the refrigerator. My hands are shaking so bad I can barely read the numbers. "Casey's number, where's Casey's number?"

"Top of the list, you bonehead." Jo's grip on the counter tightens. "And while you're at it, grab the go-bag from the hall closet."

I dial with trembling fingers, pacing back and forth like a caged animal while Casey's phone rings. *Come on, come on, pick up.*

"McKendrick residence calling for Casey," I blurt out the second someone answers.

"Clay? It's Casey. Is Jo in labor?"

"Her water broke, and she's having contractions, and the baby's not supposed to come for another week, and I don't know what to do and—"

"Clay, take a breath and exhale slowly." Casey's voice is calm and professional, as if she often coaches men whose wives are in labor. "How far apart are the contractions?"

I look helplessly at Jo, who's now leaning forward with both hands on the counter with her face scrunched up.

"We haven't been timing them," I admit, feeling utterly useless.

Jo opens one eye to glare at me. "About seven minutes. They started this morning, but I thought they were just practice ones."

My jaw drops. "This morning? Jo, why didn't you—"

"Because I knew you'd act exactly like this," she snaps, then winces as another wave of pain hits her.

Casey's calm voice comes through the speaker. "That's still early labor, but with her water breaking, I need you to bring her to the birthing center now. Don't panic, but don't dawdle either."

"Yes, ma'am." I hang up and race across the kitchen in two strides, wrapping my arm around Jo's waist. "Casey says we need to get to the birthing center."

"No kidding," Jo snaps, but then she leans into me, letting me take some of her weight. That scares me more than anything—Jo never admits when she needs help.

"The bag," she reminds me through gritted teeth.

"Right. The bag." I help her get to a chair and sit down. Then I sprint to the hall closet where the meticulously packed hospital bag has been waiting for weeks. Jo had organized it with military precision while I watched, bewildered by the sheer number of items a tiny human apparently needs.

When I return, Jo is standing up again with one hand lodged at her hip. The other hand is braced against the wall.

"Truck keys," she hisses, and I'm already grabbing them from the hook by the door.

"Got 'em, darlin'." I sling the bag over my shoulder and move to help her again, but she waves me off.

"I can still walk, Clay. I'm not made of glass."

Famous last words, because halfway to the truck, another contraction hits her like a freight train. Jo doubles over, gripping my arm so tightly I'm pretty sure she's cutting off circulation. Through clenched teeth she admits, "Okay, maybe I need a little help."

I scoop her up before she can protest, carrying her the rest of the way to the truck. I'm struck by how fragile she feels in my arms.

"Clay, put me down," Jo protests, but there's no real fight in her voice. "I am not an invalid."

"Humor me." I navigate the gravel driveway with my precious cargo in my arms and deposit her as gently as possible into the passenger seat of my truck.

She winces again.

"Another one, Jo?"

She shakes her head. "Just uncomfortable. This baby's sitting right on my—"

"Got it," I interrupt, slamming her door and sprinting around to the driver's side.

The last thing I need is another anatomy lesson. Jo's been, ah, very forthcoming about all the gory details of pregnancy because she wants to make sure I'm "properly educated about the female body." As if a lifetime of living on a ranch hadn't already taught me plenty about birth. Okay, maybe I only know about birthing horses and cows. But I don't have time to worry about that. I fire up the engine and pull out of our driveway like we're fleeing a wildfire, gravel spitting behind us.

"Clay McKendrick, if you don't slow this truck down, I swear I'll have this baby right here on your new leather seats." Jo's voice has taken on a dangerous edge, the one that reminds me she used to break wild horses for fun.

I ease off the gas, my knuckles white against the steering wheel. "Sorry, darlin'. Just trying to get you there quick."

She grunts. "I'd rather arrive alive than quick." Jo shifts uncomfortably, then sucks in a sharp breath. "Oh God, here comes another one."

I reach over to offer my hand. She grabs it and squeezes so hard I think my fingers might snap.

"Holy heaven, Jo." Though I wince, I don't pull away. I've been stomped on by thousand-pound bulls that hurt less than her grip right now.

Jo bites her lip, her forehead wrinkling. "Clay, I don't think we're gonna make it to the birthing center."

"What do you mean we're not gonna make it?" My voice jumps up an octave as I glance between her and the road. "We've got another forty minutes at least."

"You don't get it," Jo says through gritted teeth. "I mean that this baby is coming faster than you rode that mechanical bull at the county fair last summer."

"That's not funny, Jo." My heart's hammering so hard I can barely hear myself think.

"Do I look like I'm joking?" She releases my hand to grip the dashboard, her knuckles white as she pants through another contraction. "Pull over. *Now*."

I swerve onto the shoulder of the empty country road. The tires kick up dust clouds as we skid to a stop. The late afternoon sun slants through the windshield, highlighting the sheen of sweat on Jo's forehead.

"Call Casey," Jo commands, already unbuckling her seatbelt with shaking hands. "Tell her we're about twenty miles out from town, just past the old Henson place."

I fumble for my phone, nearly dropping it twice before managing to hit redial. Casey answers on the second ring.

"Jo says the baby's coming now," I blurt out. "We're pulled over on County Road 22, and I don't know what to—"

"Put me on speaker," Casey interrupts, her voice calm but urgent.

I hit the speaker button and place the phone on the dashboard. "You're on with Jo."

"Okay. Jo, honey, I need you to tell me how close your contractions are..." Casey and Jo have a brief discussion about that, then she turns back to me. "You won't make it to town, Clay."

Aw, shit. "Hang in there, Jo. It'll be okay."

"Listen to me very carefully," Casey's voice crackles through the speaker. "You're going to help Jo deliver this baby. I'm going to talk you through it, but I need you to stay calm."

My ears are ringing, probably because I stopped breathing. But I won't let Jo down, not with our baby about to pop out. Casey gives me instructions, and I follow them precisely. Ten minutes later, the most beautiful sound in the world echoes through the truck—the crying of a baby. "We did it, Jo! You and me, we brought our daughter into the world together."

My wife is exhausted but happy, based on her crooked smile. "Let me see her, Clay, please."

I carefully transfer our squalling, slippery daughter into Jo's waiting arms, marveling at how something so tiny could've caused such a commotion. The baby's face is scrunched and red, and her tiny fists are waving in protest at being evicted from her cozy home.

"She's perfect," I choke out, my vision blurring. I'm not ashamed to admit I'm crying. "Ten fingers, ten toes, and lungs like a rodeo announcer."

Casey's voice rings out from her phone. "It's a girl? Is that what you said, Clay?"

"Yes, you have a niece." I kiss Jo's forehead. "We picked the name months ago. Our daughter is Leah Mae McKendrick."

We will have an enormous party to celebrate our daughter's birth, but not today. Right now, Jo needs rest, and we both need to snuggle with our sweet baby girl. This is the best happily ever after we could have imagined.

And our lives will only get better.

If you loved

don't miss the rest of the All-American Men series!

Visit
AnnaDurand.com

to subscribe to her newsletter
for updates on forthcoming books in this series
and to receive a free gift for signing up!

Anna Durand is a bestselling, multi-award-winning author of contemporary and paranormal romance. Her books have earned bestseller status on every major retailer and wonderful reviews from readers around the world. But that's the boring spiel. Here are the really cool things you want to know about Anna!

Born on Lackland Air Force Base in Texas, Anna grew up moving here, there, and everywhere thanks to her dad's job as an instructor pilot. She's lived in Texas (twice), Mississippi, California (twice), Michigan (twice), and Alaska—and now Ohio.

As for her writing, Anna has always invented stories in her head, but she didn't write them down until her teen years. Those first awful books went into the trash can a few years later, though she learned a lot from those stories. Eventually, she would pen her first romance novel, the paranormal romance *Willpower*, and she's never looked back since.

To get exclusive content, join Anna's Facebook group, Anna's Romance Addicts, or sign up for her newsletter.

VISIT ANNADURAND.COM TO SIGN UP.